D0398756

ESCAPE FROM THE PIPE MEN!

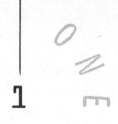

1

"Ry-an." **The Pipe Man** spoke from its square silverish mouth near the ground, below all sixteen of its many-shaded purple eyes. The eyes were set in a vertical row down its tall, thin, body, a perfectly round, gray cylinder that made it look exactly like a giant, living pipe. I recognized this Pipe Man from the many times it had visited me in my zoo sector. Next to it, a little Pipe Man, only five eyes tall, stared at me with all five eyes wide open.

"Hon-tri-ᵽuм," I said to the tall one. I smiled at them, trying to open my lips wide in a square shape, the way they did.

The five-eyed Pipe Man smiled back at me.

Hon-tri-ᵽuм blinked all sixteen of its eyes at the same time. It always blinked more than the others. I got the impression that it was thinking, really trying to study me.

"What's your name?" I asked the little one, using their language.

The little one angled all five eyes upward and blinked at Hon-tri-bum. I wondered what their relationship was. All the many times Hon-tri-bum had come to visit me before, it had been alone.

"Go on," Hon-tri-bum said.

The little one looked back at me. It closed all of its eyes at once, then opened them again. All of its eyes were bright blue.

Hon-tri-bum's top two eyes squinted, and its top several inches scrunched together like they were made of dough. I recognized the Pipe Man laughter.

"It's scared. It has never seen a member of a From species before today." To the Pipe Men, everyone who wasn't a Pipe Man was a From. Hon-tri-bum turned to face its little friend. "It won't hurt you. Anyway, it can't get out. See?" It faced me again and leaned the top of its body toward me, exposing the faint pinkness inside the mouthlike opening. Though when they were standing up straight, their tops looked like hollow round holes, they were surprisingly malleable. The Pipe Men could open and close these holes like mouths. You could say they actually had two mouths, the one at the bottom of their bodies, which they spoke out of, and the one at the top, which they used to pick things up and eat. Of course, they called eating ᐃrinkinᒡ, since they had no teeth and ate only their special soup. Now Hon-tri-þυʌ rapped the outer edge of its top-hole gently against the invisible glass, making a slight ringing sound. When it lifted its top-hole up again, it left a tiny white line of drool that seemed to hang on nothing in the air.

As the two Pipe Men stood there watching me from outside the glass, I felt the cold brushing of the message wind across my back. It was saying that it was time for dinner, time to go home.

I took three even steps backward and raised my hands above my head.

Hon-tri-þυʌ made a sucking sound and bent its top-hole toward the little one. The little one hopped a little and stretched out vertically, making its five eyes separate from one another.

I almost laughed, but caught myself. I could not ruin the departure ritual. I stood up on my tiptoes, closed my eyes, and pursed my lips. Then I brought my hands sharply down and pinned them to my sides. I bowed forward at the waist, as far as I could go. After a lot of practice, I was now able to make my head almost touch my legs. With my head still down, I shuffled backward as quickly as I could. After I had put the appropriate distance between myself and the Pipe Men, I pivoted 180 degrees, stood up straight, and walked at a respectfully slow pace toward the portal.

A minute later, I felt the light shock of the portal as I passed through it, and then the change in the texture of the air. The portal, now behind me, was black and solid-looking. You couldn't see through it from either side, but if you touched it, your hand would pass right through. I was now in the closet in my living room, in my house at 362 Ash Street, Forest Hill, Oregon, United States of America, Earth.

"Ryan!" It was my mom, calling from the kitchen.

"I'm back!" I yelled. I opened the closet door and walked out into the living room.

My seven-year-old sister, Becky, was sitting on the couch, watching TV. It was a Pipe Man show. Becky was just starting to learn their language, so she was watching it in English. I heard the female announcer's lilting computer-translated voice.

"Sleep is no wasted time with idle dreaming for the

Masters. The Masters perform a miraculous wealth of complex tasks while sleeping, including valuable scientific research . . ."

"Becky," Mom called, "go ahead and pause that for now. You can finish it tomorrow. It's time for dinner."

Becky rolled her eyes at me, and I laughed. We had both seen the same show a million times. The Pipe Men made all the Froms in the zoo watch each show a certain number of times, and all the shows had to be played in the right order. After the first few times, it got a little old.

In the kitchen, Mom had laid out our dinner on the table. Dad was standing next to his chair. I didn't need to see him because I had already smelled him from the living room. He stank with a weird metallic odor.

"Hey, Dad," I said. "How were the rats today?"

Mom frowned. "Call them Brocine, honey."

Dad shook his head. "Well, they were their usual uninteresting selves. Lying around and doing nothing. After a second week in that sector, I understand even less why the Masters care about them. I guess it's not for me to say, though."

"Maybe they'll have you go back to the Horn-Puffs soon," said Mom.

"Oh, that would be great," said Dad. "Did you know, the Horn-Puffs eat only a single species of soft-bodied insect? Just one thing, every day for their whole lives."

Becky snickered, and I tried to hold back a smile. Dad had made that same comment almost every night he'd come home from working in the Horn-Puff sector. After all that talk, I almost wanted to try one of these "soft-bodied insects" myself, just to see what all the fuss was about.

"Now, take your places before it gets cold," said Mom.

Becky and I got behind our assigned chairs, and Mom laid the final dish down on the table before taking her place. She nodded at us.

We all turned abruptly around and raised our arms over our heads. Then we brought our arms down, tight against our bodies, and bowed low.

"For all we have, we thank them," said Mom. "For all we are, we owe them. For all they ask, we give them." Mom clapped her hands together once.

In unison, Dad, Becky, and I lifted our heads up, jumped 180 degrees, pulled our chairs out, and sat down.

2

WE WEREN'T SUPPOSED TO LOOK at the Pipe Men spectators who stood outside the glass while we were inside doing lessons with our Pipe Men tutors, and we weren't allowed to talk to the spectators until it was time for the afternoon performance. But now that I was getting fluent in their language, it was impossible not to overhear.

"On top they are called arms, and on the bottom, legs," said a short one with only eight eyes. I recognized this one from the many times it had come by our sector and given the same speech. "Since they have no assistants, they need these extra pipes to move and drink."

The spectators murmured. I could feel the dozens of eyes on me. It made it hard to concentrate on the math lesson that Yel-to-tor, my tutor, was giving me.

The equations were hard enough without people talking about my body parts while I was trying to work. I let out a sigh of frustration.

"Let me see," said Yel-to-tor.

I pushed my notebook toward the Pipe Man and twisted it around so it could see.

Yel-to-tor bent its top four pea-green eyes over my paper. Then it bent all the way over the table and picked up my pencil with its top-hole. "Here." It tapped my equation with the pencil. "This is a material transposition of the primary and final variables. You should not still be making this mistake."

"What?" I was learning the mathematical terms as we went along, and I had never learned them in English. I had to not only figure out what material transposition and all that meant, but also keep all the inflections and pronunciations straight. I sighed again.

Yel-to-tor scrunched its top-hole around the pencil and let out a wheezing rush of air. It made a sound like the wings of a bird flapping. The tutor set the pencil on the table, and where it had been inside the Pipe Man's top-hole, it was covered in light white drool. "It's almost time for your performance. We will do this again tomorrow." Yel-to-tor propelled away from me. Like all Pipe Men, it moved by hovering above the ground and floating on a jet of air that it expelled from the bottom of its pipelike body. As it propelled, the edges of its bottom-hole wrinkled with effort and flapped a little with the jet of air. Yel-to-tor propelled toward the door that led through the invisible glass barrier, out into the viewing lane. I wouldn't have known the door was there if I hadn't seen the Pipe Men go through it, since it was as invisible as the rest of our cage. Yel-to-tor tapped on the air once with its top-hole, waited a second, and then propelled through.

Becky had been working with her tutor, Bre-zon-air, at a table a few yards away from us. Now she came walking across our sector, her feet squishing into the rubbery artificial ground. We both had to wear special boots to keep from bouncing and slipping. Lately, she'd been working on language for two hours every morning.

"I learned how to say 'You make good soup!'" Becky said as she reached me.

"Thank you, you also make a pleasant brew," I said, bowing low.

Becky bowed back at me and giggled.

"Bless my eyes, it can speak!" said a Pipe Man from outside the glass. It had ten eyes and was as wide-eyed as the little five-eyed one had been the day before.

"Amazing," said its companion. "Look—they are about to drink."

While we'd been working with our tutors, Mom had come back from the Pipe Man soup kitchen to make us some human food. Two sandwiches were sitting on two regular human plates, on a small table right in front of the invisible glass.

Several more Pipe Men joined the two who were already watching us.

Becky and I threw our hands up, then bowed down, facing the spectators.

"They're so amazed by how we eat," said Becky, taking her seat.

"I guess you'd find us interesting, too, if you had no teeth and all you 'drank' was soup," I said.

Just above the top of the tallest Pipe Man, several wires were strung over the lane. They moved slowly, pulling along containers shaped like little teapots. Every once in a while, one of the wires would stop moving, and one of the teapots would pour its contents into the open top-hole of a spectator. That was all we knew of Pipe Man eating habits.

"What is that you're drinking?" asked a spectator with only six eyes.

"When we drink something solid, we call it eating," I said. "It's called a sandwich."

"Sandwich," said Six-eyes. It pressed its eyes against the glass, distorting its features.

I opened my mouth wide and showed my teeth, then took an exaggerated bite. This caused three more spectators to press their eyes up against the glass.

Becky giggled at them and waved.

We both kept eating, taking large bites and chewing obscenely. If we'd done this at dinner with Mom and Dad, Mom would have given us the death stare. But here, we were supposed to exaggerate everything. I swallowed my last bite, pushed away from the table, and stood up.

"Oh!" a Pipe Man exclaimed.

"Becky, let's exercise our appendages!" I said. Becky knew this Pipe Man phrase because we'd practiced it. We were supposed to act as if this was how humans normally behaved, never mind the fact that, of course, no one else on Earth knew Pipe Men existed, much less spoke their language.

Becky stood up, leaving a bit of sandwich on the plate. Three of the Pipe Men leaned toward it, top-holes dripping tiny amounts of drool. Their eyes blinked rapidly in succession. The rest of the Pipe Men pointed all their eyes toward us.

"One, two," I chanted, kicking a leg up, then punching an arm out.

"One, two!" Becky shouted. She jumped in the air, raising her arms.

"One, two, three!" I cried, bouncing on one leg and kicking the other leg out. I had to wave my arms to keep steady.

"Dance!" Becky cried. She began running around me in a circle, pumping her fists up in the air.

"That's not dancing!" I said.

"You dance, I run!" she puffed, making another round.

"Dance," I said very slowly, for the Pipe Men's benefit. Then I stood up on my toes like a ballerina, touched my hand to my head, and slowly twirled.

"Hoof, hoof, hoof!" the Pipe Men chanted. The

word didn't really translate. All I knew was, it was some kind of expression of approval.

When she got back around in front of me, Becky stopped and reached out a hand for our special hopping-together show. The Pipe Men loved it. But then Becky's face turned pale.

"What?" I turned to see what she was looking at.

Mom was rushing toward us from the portal that led to our Earth house. She was crying.

"Mom! What's wrong?"

"Ryan . . ." Mom was sobbing so hard that I didn't understand anything except my name.

"What is it, Mom?"

". . . the Brocine . . . poisoned noses . . ."

"Is it Dad?" Becky burst into tears too.

"Mom, what happened?" I asked.

"One of the Brocine babies poked him with its nose. It jabbed him with its spike out of nowhere. He—he's alive, but he won't wake up."

"Where is he now?" I was aware of all the Pipe Men still watching us. Even more had crowded around since Mom had come running out. They didn't make any noise, just stared at us, rapt.

"Our parent was hurt in an accident," I said to them. "Mom, where is he?"

"He's in the ward. The hospital. He won't wake up."

"But you said he's alive. They're helping him, right?" I asked.

Mom nodded and wiped her eyes.

"Then we'll go see him. If they're working on him, I'm sure he'll be fine. I bet he's even waking up right now."

Mom seemed to get herself together a little. She took Becky's hand and nodded at me, eyes wet. Becky and I weren't supposed to leave our zoo sector during the day. In fact, we weren't supposed to leave our zoo sector at all, unless it was just to go back to our house. In our hurry, we even turned our backs to the Pipe Men, forgetting all about the ritual.

3

TO GET TO ANY PLACE BESIDES our zoo sector on O-thul-ba, the Pipe Man planet, we had to go back into our house through the living room closet, and then into the closet in Mom and Dad's bedroom. Their closet led into a passageway. I'd only been in there a few times before, and that was right after the Pipe Men came, when I was younger than Becky. Dad had told me never to go back without him or Mom. He'd said that I would get lost and never find my way home, *and* we'd get in trouble with the Masters. So far, I'd been too scared to disobey him.

I hesitated at the bedroom doorway. "Did they say it was okay to bring us?" We were only going to go to a different part of O-thul-ba, not to any of the From planets, but still, I didn't want to get in trouble.

"I didn't think to ask about it," said Mom.

"Do you know where the hospital is?"

Mom sniffed. "My daughter was born there. It's not something you forget." She squeezed Becky's hand. "Come on, we're all going to go see him." She walked into the closet and through the blackness at the back, pulling Becky with her.

Even with what had happened, I was excited to be going into the passage. Maybe we'd run into some new Froms. Dad had met a lot of them and described them to me, and of course we had TV from lots of planets, but it wasn't the same as seeing them in person. I followed Mom and Becky through the closet.

The passage was just as I remembered it. It was wide enough for two people to walk together, and the places where the floor and ceiling met the walls were rounded rather than right angles. The ground was pinkish and soft, and instead of a wall in front of me, there was a rectangular black space. It was not quite static but moved a little, swirling ever so slightly with many varied shades of black. When I turned around, I could see the rectangular black door that we had come through, also swirling a little. Along both walls, there were other black doors, spaced maybe five feet apart. In between the doors, the walls were the same pinkish color as the ground. A soft, white light illuminated us, seeming to come from nowhere and everywhere at once.

I could tell that Becky was excited to be here, too, because she had stopped crying and was standing with her mouth open. As far as I knew, she had never been in here since she was a baby.

Mom started walking briskly, pulling Becky along. As we passed each of the black doorways, I couldn't tell one apart from another. It was only a minute before I had completely lost track of which one led to our house. But Mom seemed to know exactly where she was going because a minute later, she abruptly stopped, cocked her head as if she was listening for something, and pulled Becky through a door.

I hesitated for a few seconds, trying to mark the spot in my mind, but as I looked back, all I saw were the doors going on in both directions, all looking exactly the same.

I came out into a different kind of hallway. Instead of the soft, fleshy floor of the passage, it had the same rubbery floor as our zoo sector. The ceiling was maybe twenty-five eyes up, tall enough to be over the head of the tallest Pipe Man. Little teapots hung limply from assistant wires suspended just under the ceiling.

"Ryan, stay with me," said Mom. She was standing with Becky in front of an open doorway.

I hurried to catch up to them.

The doorway was tall and thin like the Pipe Men. We would have to go through it one by one, sideways. Beyond that were rows of long, narrow tables, all empty.

"Is that where the Pipe Men sleep?" asked Becky.

"Only when they're sick," said Mom. She hesitated for a second.

"Mom, are we supposed to be here?" I asked. I didn't see anything human, and I was suddenly afraid. I had never seen a Pipe Man except from inside our sector. I had no idea what they'd do.

"They told me he was back here," said Mom. "Did they expect us to just wait and hope they know what to do with a sick human?"

"What are we going to do, kidnap him?" I asked. "What would Earth doctors know about from poison anyway?"

"I'm not going to kidnap him," said Mom. "I just

need to find out if they can help him." Mom slid sideways through the door and into the room, still pulling Becky. At first, there was enough space to walk normally, but the passage between the tables gradually narrowed, so much that Mom had to slide sideways again. But she moved quickly. She was used to moving this way, since she worked all day in the Pipe Men soup kitchens.

Becky was having a little more trouble. "Ow, Mom, not so fast!"

I wasn't used to this either, since I'd never been allowed into real Pipe Men spaces before, but I managed to follow them without bumping into the tables too many times. The room with the rows of empty tables went on for quite a while. Assistant wires ran all across the ceiling, ready to provide anything the Pipe Men needed. Here and there, strangely shaped instruments hung from the wires along with the soup pots. Finally, Mom reached another hallway and we were in front of another long, thin doorway.

"Where does this go?" asked Becky.

"To the From part of the hospital." Mom's voice sounded bitter, but I didn't want to disturb her by asking about it. I just followed them through. We were now in a place that looked much like a human hospital. The room was bigger, with real beds laid out in rows, separated by curtains. It looked like some of the beds were filled, but I couldn't see anything but blurry shapes behind the curtains.

Several Pipe Men stood next to one of the curtains. All their eyes turned toward us.

"How did they get in here?" one of them asked.

"The parent must know the way."

"They must be sent back."

Two of the Pipe Men glided toward us. Both were tall, at least sixteen eyes each.

"Earth family. You have heard about Os-car's illness," said one.

"Where is it?" Mom asked. She meant Dad. The Pipe Men didn't have words for male and female, husband or wife. She was shaking a little, but she looked right at the Pipe Man. "Is that it there?" She pointed at the curtain surrounding the nearest bed, where the other Pipe Men were still watching us.

One of the Pipe Men back at the bed blinked only its top eye. I had never seen any of them do that before. The two Pipe Men with us turned around so that their eyes were facing away from us, and the Pipe Man by the bed blinked its top eye again. Then it blinked one a few eyes down, then other ones, quickly, one after the other. The two Pipe Men near us abruptly turned around again.

"You will be allowed to see it," one said. They separated from each other, leaving a space between them big enough for us to walk through in the normal way.

Mom didn't wait for any more instructions. She pulled Becky forward, and I followed them. The two Pipe Men fell in behind us, blocking the exit.

I didn't recognize any of the Pipe Men outside the curtain. That meant that if they'd ever been to see us, they weren't regulars. I'd learned to recognize the ones I saw a lot, like Hon-tri-bum.

The curtain opened as we came toward it, pulled along assistant wires, and I saw my dad lying on a bed. Above and around the bed were more assistant wires, much like the ones that were strung across the ceiling, only these were not parallel with each other but intertwined in a strange pattern. Two were connected to Dad, one in his jaw and the other in his stomach.

Mom sobbed and ran toward him, brushing past the Pipe Men. "Oh, Oscar!" She turned back toward us. "What are you doing for it? What are these wires for?"

The Pipe Men blinked at each other. Finally, the one nearest to Mom spoke.

"We are keeping it alive."

Mom stood up and planted herself right in front of the Pipe Man who'd been speaking. "You can't help it. I need to take it back to Earth."

"You cannot take it outside your home."

"I'll tell them it was a snake bite. An Earth animal. Or I'll tell them I just don't know. Let them do what they can. You don't know enough about us!"

Several wires untwined themselves from the pattern above Dad's bed and lowered themselves between Mom and the Pipe Man. They hung in front of her, taut, blocking her path back to Becky and me.

"You will stay here," said the Pipe Man. It turned all its eyes toward Becky and me.

I wasn't sure what to do. Were they really going to make Mom stay here? I knew what our parents had taught us. When in doubt, do the ritual. I had already been holding on to Becky's hand. Now I lifted both my hands up, and Becky followed. We bowed as low as we could go.

"We will send a from to watch the children." The Pipe Man turned to one of its fellows. "Take them back."

It blinked at another one of the Pipe Men, who floated away past the other silent curtains.

Mom stood frozen behind the wires, tears flowing down her cheeks. Still looking at us, she grabbed one of Dad's listless hands.

"We'll be okay, Mom," I said. I tried not to let my voice show how fast my heart was beating. The Pipe Men had never done anything like this before. None of us had ever been really sick before, either. "You take care of Dad. We'll be fine."

Becky moved like she was going to go to Mom, but I held her hand firmly. "We're going back with this Pipe Man. Mom's going to be fine. Dad needs her. Do you understand?"

Becky was crying, but she nodded.

The Pipe Man who had floated away floated back now. It carried some kind of device in its top-hole that looked like a thin, jagged rock. Light spilled out of the top of the device, giving the Pipe Man a little halo. Its fellow closed its top-hole and then, with a coughing sound, spit up a black pen-like instrument. It gripped the slimy stylus with its top-hole, then blinked at me.

I bowed my head.

"This way," it said. It turned back the way we'd come

and began to glide over the rubbery floor. The one with the strange device followed it.

I glanced back at Mom. She was still standing rigid in front of the wires, gripping Dad's hand, but she nodded at me. I tried not to look at Dad, but I couldn't help it. He lay there looking an inch from death. I quickly turned back and followed the Pipe Men, gripping Becky's hand.

4

THE PIPE MAN WITH THE STYLUS tapped the other Pipe Man's device. I couldn't tell what that did, but after a few seconds, the Pipe Men silently began leading us down the passage. They stopped in front of one of the doors that looked the same as all the others.

The one with the stylus peered at the device with its top eye. "Here," it said.

I faced them and nudged Becky. We raised our arms up, brought them sharply down, and backed through the door. With a slight buzz, we were back in Mom and Dad's closet. The bedroom was eerily quiet, all the more so because I almost never came into this room.

As soon as we got through the door, Becky bolted into the living room, plopped down on the couch, and started sobbing.

I felt the same way, but I wasn't going to let her see it. I sat down next to her. "Come on, he's going to be fine. Look at what the Pipe Men can do. They have assistants, not just the wires but all sorts of other machines that Earth people don't have. They have spaceships, and they can open up a door to our house even though they're a gazillion miles away. They can take care of a little poison."

Becky went on crying, and I put my arms around her. None of us had been treated by a Pipe Man doctor since Becky was born. They had studied us, taken weird scans with some kind of alien machine. But what did they really know? They didn't even understand arms and legs. I patted Becky on the back, then leaned over to the window behind us and pushed the curtain aside, just a little bit. It was still sunny outside, and with my eyes used to the dimness of O-thυl-þa, it seemed too bright.

A woman was walking by on the sidewalk. She saw me and stopped cold, staring. I quickly pulled the curtain shut, heart beating fast. She was the first human outside my family I'd seen in weeks.

"What if they don't let her come back?" Becky asked, still sobbing a little.

"They're going to let her. Once Dad gets well, they'll

both come back." I hadn't liked the way they'd acted toward her either. She was just trying to help Dad. What if they *didn't* let her come back?

"Why won't they let him go to a doctor?"

"It's how they're always worried about the Earth people knowing about them. Some Earth doctor might find the poison and guess it was caused by another Froм. That's what they're worried about." That explanation didn't quite make sense to me, though. No one else on Earth even knew other Froмs existed. They didn't even have real spaceships. How would they guess?

"But we go outside sometimes."

It was true, we did go outside sometimes. We'd even been to the doctor's. But not often, and always with Mom or Dad. We were taught not to trust Earth people.

"This is different," I said. "We can't take anything from other planets out there."

Just as I got finished talking, there was a rattling inside the living room closet, the one that led to our zoo sector. Something banged on the inside of the door. Becky sat frozen, shocked out of her sobs.

"Hello?" I said.

"Hello?" said a voice.

"Who is it?"

"Ip. How do I get this thing open?"

Ip. I tried to remember where I'd heard that name.

"Your parent calls me a Horn-Puff," said the voice. "Now, help me get out of here before I suffocate!"

A Horn-Puff! In our house? I rushed over to the closet and pulled the door open. There he was, looking just the way Dad had described them. He was about twice the size of Dad, though not much taller, soft-looking and blobby. He was colored mostly a light green, with white blobs here and there that peeled like a skin rash. Only his skin was nothing like ours. It was dewy and shimmery, even in the dimness of the closet. Only the white patches were dry. He had pupil-less eyes like giant pomegranate rinds.

"Ip!" I cried. "They let you come to our planet?"

"Someone had to watch you children." The Horn-Puff stepped out of the closet and into the living room, turning his blobby head on his nonexistent neck. "Interesting place you've got here. What's over there?" Ip globbed his way over to the window behind the couch. He moved slowly, but surprisingly well for having very poorly defined legs. A single thick, woody white horn protruded from the middle of his back, ending in a sharp point that glimmered like the Horn-Puff's skin. He pushed the curtain aside with a swipe of one blobby arm.

"Oh . . ." Ip stood perfectly still, staring out.

"You can't do that!" I rushed over to him and pulled the curtain shut. Fortunately, it seemed like no one was out there anymore. "What if someone sees you?"

"What are you talking about? I don't understand!" Becky had stopped crying and was glaring up at me accusingly.

"I told him he can't go around looking out people's windows on other planets. No one's supposed to know you exist!"

"They won't believe it. One time, a Hippt child went wandering right into Hdkowl, my planet. Everyone acted like it was a hgso!"

"I don't know what a Hippt or a hgso is, but you can't count on Earth people being that stupid!"

"Mfff," said Ip. "You have anything to drink?"

"We're all out of insects," I said.

"Urg. Well, you children stay here. I'll be right back after dinner." With that, Ip blobbed his way across the room, stuffed himself back into the closet, and was gone.

Becky was still glaring at me.

"Come on," I said, "you must have understood some of that."

"A little. I know he said he had to eat. I'm hungry too."

"We just had lunch." I was hungry too, though, so I went with Becky into the kitchen. Unfortunately, the refrigerator was almost empty, and so were the cupboards. I sighed. I didn't know when Mom was coming back, and the From who ate only one kind of insect wasn't going to be much help. If Becky and I were going to eat, we were going to have to go to the store. I went over to the cookie jar where Mom kept her stash of Earth money.

"Ryan! You can't go out there!" Becky looked horrified.

"What am I supposed to do, go back and ask the Pipe Men for some soup?"

Becky wrinkled her nose.

"Exactly! I'm going to have to go out there. And I'm not going to leave you alone here, so that means you're coming, too."

I thought she was going to start crying again.

"No," I said, taking her shoulders. "It's not going

to be like last time. We'll change our clothes. I'm sure we've got something that will pass." I looked down at my shimmering black tunic that looked vaguely like a shiny potato sack and square-toed boots made from the skin of an O-thʊl-ban Id-won. I'd seen enough TV to know that this wasn't what the other kids were wearing.

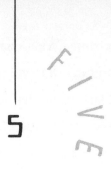

5

"WHAT DO YOU THINK?" Becky came out of her room wearing a gray dress. It came down a little below her knees, and the sleeves went barely past her elbows. It didn't give her much shape.

"Don't you have any jeans?"

"They're too small." She held up a tiny pair of jeans against her waist.

I sighed. I had managed to squeeze into a pair of jeans, but they were way too short. At least I'd found a T-shirt that fit okay. Fortunately, Mom had recently brought home some Earth shoes for both of us. I didn't know if they were in fashion, but at least we'd be able to make it to the store and back.

I helped Becky put on her sneakers. With the thick boot socks she was wearing, they almost didn't fit. But these were the socks we wore every day, and we didn't have any others. At least my socks covered the part of my legs that the too-short pant legs didn't. I helped her to her feet.

"Ready?"

Becky stared at the door and shook her head.

"I know. Me neither." I held her hand, turned the doorknob, and slowly pushed the door open. There was the front porch, then three steps leading down to a paved walkway through a patch of tidy grass, and at the end of that, a sidewalk. Beyond that was a street, empty except for a few parked cars. The sun was shining brightly down on all of it.

I fumbled with the key in my hand, checking it in the lock to make sure it was the right one before I closed the door behind us. Becky was still gripping me hard, and she was shaking a little.

"It's going to be fine," I said. "I've been to this store twice with Mom. It's . . ." Where was it? I tried to act like I was just enjoying the sunshine instead of trying to fig-ure out which way to go. "That way." I started walking, pulling Becky along, all the way through the yard and to the sidewalk. I wanted to keep moving before either I lost my nerve or Becky started crying.

"Hey!" a voice called.

I didn't look and kept walking.

"Hey! Ryan!" My heart leapt. Who would know me? I heard footsteps behind me and realized I couldn't avoid facing this.

"You're Ryan Hawthorn, right?" The kid had caught up to us, walking on the other side of Becky, on the small strip of grass between the sidewalk and the street.

Becky pulled closer to me.

"And you're Becky, right?"

Becky stared back at him.

It was just a regular kid, probably a little younger than me, maybe eleven or twelve. I tried to keep calm.

"Yeah, that's right. Hi," I said.

"Don't you remember me? I live right there." The kid pointed back toward where we had come from, but I couldn't tell what house he was pointing at. Our house was disturbingly far away now.

"Oh, yeah," I said. He did look a little bit familiar. Maybe he was someone I used to play with before the Pipe Men came. There'd been a few kids on this street. I tried to place his name, but it didn't come to me.

"Well, my mom always says, you know, if you ever

see those kids next door, be nice and invite them over 'cause they must not have a lot of friends what with being homeschooled and all."

"Thanks," I said. "That's really nice of you, but we're just going to the store really quick for our mom. We have to get back." I picked up the pace a little.

"Okay, whatever," said the kid. He stopped still and let us go.

I took a quick glance behind us and saw him standing there looking confused.

"Who was that?" Becky whispered.

"I don't know. The kid next door, I guess." I paused. It was bothering me that I didn't remember his name. I felt like I should know him. But I tried to shake it off for Becky. She'd never had any Earth friends. To her, Earth was even stranger than it was for me. "Hey, he didn't make fun of our clothes, right? It's not so bad being out here."

Becky didn't answer.

I scanned the street ahead of us, desperately trying to remember which way to go. All the houses looked the same. All the intersections were marked by the same big red signs showing the word STOP in giant letters. But

I knew that if I went left, I'd get to the bigger street. I hoped I'd know where to go from there. Fortunately, no one else stopped us.

As we approached the main street, a car barreled around the corner.

Becky yelped.

"It's just a car," I said. "You know, a machine. That's why we stay out of the street."

"It's like an assistant?"

"Yeah, just like that." I looked up and down the street and sighed with relief. "Come on, it's down there."

More cars passed us going both directions as we walked. They seemed so noisy, so chaotic. The Pipe Men had assistants that carried them from place to place. My tutor, Yel-to-tor, had shown me a video. They moved smoothly, noiselessly, over the dim, smooth O-thul-ban ground. I was happy to pull Becky into the little store and out of the bright street.

As we walked in, the man behind the counter looked me up and down. His eyes rested on my pant legs, then narrowed. Becky noticed and pulled closer to me. I hurriedly grabbed a basket and started throwing things in. They didn't have a wide selection, so I just went with anything edible. After a few minutes, I had bread, Chef

Boyardee, soup, canned vegetables, pasta, pretzels, chips, marshmallows, and cheese.

"Mom's not going to be happy with me for feeding you this," I said. As I picked through my unhealthy selections, Becky handed me a six-pack of Hershey's chocolate bars. For the first time since we'd come in here, she smiled. I put it in my basket. Mom could yell at me if she wanted to. I just hoped I had enough money. I didn't know how I was going to get more unless they'd let me talk to Mom.

I put the basket on the counter. The man stared at me suspiciously. He hadn't taken his eyes off us the entire time.

"I have money," I said, pulling the wad of cash out of my pocket.

The man's expression didn't change, but he started ringing my stuff up.

A woman with two kids came into the store. One of the kids was a girl Becky's age, the other a boy who looked about ten. The girl stared at us and poked her brother. He laughed. Becky pressed her lips together like she was holding back tears. Through the glass door, I could see that the sun was starting to go down.

"Fifty-eight oh nine," said the man.

I tried to separate the bills and count it out. Five, ten, thirty, I thought. I finished counting out the total. "Here you go."

The man pulled his head back and opened his eyes wide.

It took me a second to realize what I'd said. "I mean, here," I said, holding out the wad of cash I'd counted.

The man hesitated before taking it, then stuffed it into the register.

I grabbed my bags of groceries and pushed Becky out the door as fast as possible. The mistake I'd made had me confused. The sidewalk didn't feel quite right under my feet. It should have been springier. My new sneakers made my feet hurt.

"It's okay," said Becky. "He'll never know what you said."

"It's not that, it's . . . just a little weird being out here."

"It's okay now that it's getting dark." Becky dropped my hand and skipped, swinging the plastic shopping bag she was carrying.

I was happy that she wasn't freaking out anymore, but I still wanted to get home as soon as possible. Every time a car passed by, I wanted to run, but I made myself walk normally. The last thing I needed was to draw more attention to us.

"Hey, look!" Becky pointed down a cross street, not the one we'd come down. In between two houses, there was a tiny playground. "Can we stop?" She didn't wait for me to answer but skipped down the street toward it.

I followed. "We have to get back. Ip could come and find us missing, and then who knows what they'll do?" I wasn't sure what the Pipe Men would do if they thought we'd run off, but I didn't want to find out.

Becky ignored me. "It's like the one we used to have in our sector before we got the rubber tree!"

It was almost exactly like that. Two swings, a wooden structure made of logs, a slide, and a metal jungle gym. The springy maze of dull black Pipe Man synthetic fabric, designed to be the perfect exercise facility for Earth children, just wasn't the same. I set down my bags.

"Okay, but just for a minute."

Becky hadn't waited for my approval and was already at the top of the slide. "Woo!" she yelled, jumping onto it, then, "Agh!" as she landed in the sawdust. "Let's swing!"

I joined her on the swing set. It looked a little rickety, but after pushing a swing back and forth a few times, I decided it would hold my weight.

"Look at the clouds!" Becky was already swinging, a big smile on her face.

Sitting still on my swing, I looked up. The sun was setting, and parts of the clouds were turning orange. They slowly moved across the sky. The amazing part was that there was something between them. A sky that went up and up and up. On O-thul-ƀa, a single large, unbroken cloud covered the entire sky. I felt like I was seeing my own planet for the first time.

"Hey!" A police car had stopped at the edge of the playground, and a short but stocky cop was walking toward us. "You the Hawthorn kids?"

Becky stopped swinging.

"Yes," I said.

"A neighbor asked me to check in on you. Seems you kids don't come out much. Just wanted to see if everything was okay." The officer glanced at our forgotten shopping bags, then let his eyes rest on my pant legs.

"We used to have a swing set just like this," said Becky.

"Is that so?" The officer smiled at her. "Where are your parents, miss?"

"They're at home waiting for us," I said. "We'd better get going." I jumped off the swing and gave Becky a look.

She climbed off.

The officer scrunched up his eyes as he took in Becky's gray dress and tennis shoes. "I can give you a ride home if you want. No trouble."

"That's okay," I said. "Thanks anyway. We really should go." I rushed past the officer and picked up our bags.

Becky followed me and tried to grab one of the bags. As she came closer, I could see tears forming in her eyes.

"It's okay," I whispered. "Thanks!" I called out to the officer. Without waiting to see what he did, we took off as fast as we could go without actually running.

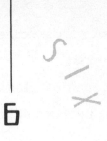

6

We didn't look behind us until we were back at our house. As I fumbled with the key, I saw that the street was empty. I wasn't going to give the cop a chance to catch up, so I pushed Becky inside.

"Where have you been?" Ip was sitting on our living room floor, his large pomegranate-like eyes staring at us accusingly. He had the TV on, watching a blank white picture. As I took in the scene, several Horn-Puffs rushed in front of the camera, and then the screen was blank again.

"We went to the store," I said. "To get nutrition."

"I brought you something," said Ip. He tipped his head, pointing to a bag on the floor, made of Pipe Man rubbery fabric. "Didn't think I'd let you starve, did you?"

I translated for Becky, and we both tried not to laugh. I wasn't sure I wanted to see what was inside the bag, but I didn't want to be rude.

Ip kept staring at me expectantly. Then a noise came from the TV. All of a sudden, a whole herd of Horn-Puffs appeared on the screen, and they all appeared to be jumping up and down frantically, waving their blobby limbs at us. Ip turned back to it, riveted.

I went over to the bag, took a deep breath, and pulled at it. The top of the bag, which had been stuck together with some kind of suction, fell open with a slurping sound. I couldn't believe my eyes. "It looks like a cake!"

"A cake?" Becky hopped over to me and peered in. "It *is* a cake!"

It was round, a foot in diameter, and looked like an ordinary birthday cake with ordinary chocolate frosting, just like Mom made.

"Ip, is this a cake?" I asked.

"What did you expect, insects?" Ip's entire body shook with a deep roaring sound that I figured must be laughter.

"Well . . ." I smiled nervously. "Yeah! I mean, where did you get a cake?"

Ip stopped laughing and looked away from me. "Helena gave it to me. It said it made it earlier today as a surprise for you children. They let it go back to the kitchen to get it for you. Helena said it was very important that you drink it."

"Mom?" Becky asked. "Mom made it?" She reached down, grabbed a fingerful of frosting, and licked it off.

"Wait until after dinner," I said. I liked Mom's cake as much as Becky did. But I didn't like that they didn't let Mom come and give it to us herself. Why couldn't they let her just come back?

Becky rolled her eyes at me, but she let me put the cake on the kitchen counter. I put our groceries away and opened up a soup can for each of us.

"What does homeschooled mean?" she asked.

"What?"

"That kid said we were homeschooled. What does it mean?"

"Well . . ." I wasn't a hundred percent sure. "I think most kids go someplace else to learn. Like we have Yel-to-tor and Bre-zon-air. Only a whole bunch of kids go there together, and they only learn Earth stuff." I had a vague memory of going to some kind of school. There was a lady with curly blond hair and a board with giant plastic letters and—

"But Bre-zon-air doesn't come to our house. We go to our zoo sector."

I tried to organize my thoughts. "They don't know that. They think Mom teaches us. They think we don't go to school because of our religion."

"What's our religion?"

"I don't know. It's just what they think. You know how we're not supposed to tell anyone about the Pipe Men and how there are other planets and everything?" I put our soup on the table.

"Yeah."

"Well, people have to think something about us, so when people ask Mom why we don't go to school, that's what she tells them."

"I thought we weren't supposed to lie." She slurped her soup.

"Sometimes you have to. I mean, what would happen if everyone knew about the Pipe Men?"

"I don't know."

I didn't know either. I'd never really thought about it. We just weren't supposed to tell anyone. There was an impression that something bad would happen, but what was it?

"Hey, Ip?"

"Uurp."

"Why aren't we supposed to tell anyone about the Masters?"

"They're afraid all the Earth people will find out that the Masters are stealing their resources. Then you Earth people would kick them out, or they'd have to get into a war."

"They're stealing our resources?"

"Oh, yes," said Ip. "On all the From planets. Probably hiding away where no one can see them, sucking up everything they can."

"Probably?" I asked. "You don't know?"

Ip rolled his blobby shoulders in a shrug. "Same everywhere."

I had the feeling these weren't the official answers. When Mom reminded us not to tell anyone, she would just say, "For all we have, we thank them."

"Can you tell the other Horn-Puffs about them?" I asked.

Ip pursed his thick, round lips. "My people know.

They fought the assistants and lost. Now the Masters take what they want without hiding."

I wanted to ask more, but Becky poked me.

"Ip says the Pipe Men steal everyone's resources, and if we tell about them, they'll start a war and take over our planet." I said to Becky.

"Why?"

I didn't know what to say, so I just ate for a minute. Mom and Dad had never said anything about the Pipe Men stealing or taking over planets. The Pipe Men were better than us. They were older, smarter. They knew everything. We did rituals to show them respect. We were the luckiest family on Earth because they'd chosen us over everyone else, and we owed them everything. Before they came, we'd been dirt poor. Dad had no job. Mom was pregnant with Becky, and we were going to lose our house. Then they came, and now we had all the food we could eat and better education than anyone on the planet. I heard Dad's satisfied tone in my head, reciting this story for the millionth time. Only now they were keeping Mom away from us, keeping Dad in their hospital even though he might die.

I tried to remember before they came, but there wasn't much. Just living in this house, flashes of playing with kids in the street. Flashes of school. It must have been preschool. And then the Pipe Men came through Mom and Dad's closet.

"I want some cake!" Becky said, showing me her empty soup bowl.

"Okay." I got up and pulled out a cake knife. I almost didn't want to eat it. What if Mom never came back to make us another one?

"Come on!" Becky hopped excitedly in her chair.

"All right, all right." I cut into it. The knife went through smoothly, and the piece I'd cut came out easily onto the plate. It looked too good for me to pass up, all moist and chocolaty and perfect. I began slicing another piece. Then the knife hit something that resisted it. I pulled the knife back and looked down at the slice mark. "Oh my gosh."

"What?"

"It looks like something's in here!"

Becky came running over and tried to peer at the cake, but she was too short to see what I was looking at.

I reached my hand into the cake to where the knife

had hit something. It felt like a sheet of Pipe Man fabric. I pulled at it, and it slid easily out of the cake into my hand.

"What *is* it?"

"It's . . . I think it's some kind of note." The fabric was almost black, but something had been etched into it. It was crude, but I could read it. I had to flip it over to read it all.

"What?"

"'Ryan and Becky: Only the Brocine have the cure for their poison. The Hottini will take you to them. Ip will know what to do. I love you. Mom. Friend Ip: It's time. Door 1064.'"

"Mom baked a note cake!" Becky slid the plate with her piece on it off the counter and eagerly began to eat. "If goot!" she said with her mouth full.

"Ip, did you know this cake had a note in it?"

Ip had come into the entrance to the kitchen. He pressed his large blobby arms together. "I thought maybe, but I wasn't sure. What does it say?"

"We have to find the Brocine so they can cure Dad. It says the 'Hottini' will take us and 'It's time.' And then it gives a door number — 1064."

"Oh." Ip wrung his blobby arms. "This isn't good. Not good."

"Why? What happened? What do you know?"

Ip sucked in so much air that my shirt puffed out and the end of my hair fell forward into my face. Then he let it out again, blowing my T-shirt and hair the other way. The remains of Becky's cake landed against her dress, and she glared at Ip.

"Tell us what you know," I said, too loudly.

"Helena wasn't able to say anything when it gave me the . . . cake? But if it wants me to take you through door 1064, then Helena must think . . ."

That Dad was about to die. Ip didn't need to say it.

Becky's eyes welled up.

"It's okay," I said. "I didn't mean to yell at Ip. Mom says we have to ask some Froms called the Hottini to take us to the Brocine. The Brocine have the cure for their poison. Dad's going to be okay."

Becky nodded.

"We'll get to see another planet. Go through some more doors. Stuff Mom never let us do before." For good reason, I thought.

Becky stuffed the rest of her cake into her mouth.

Whatever we had to do now, I didn't want her to freak out. She wasn't going to believe it was all fun and games, but at least I could try to make her feel safe.

"You are going to help us, right?" I asked Ip.

Ip's eyes sucked a little way back into his head. "You know what they do when they catch you going against them?"

"What? They're already going to let Dad..." I didn't want Becky to hear the rest of it. She sometimes understood more than she let on.

"They cut you off, that's what! You'll never be able to come back to Earth! I'll never be able to go back to Hdkowl."

I felt like I was going to cry too. "I can't find this door by myself, or these Hottini, whoever they are. You must know more about all this than I do."

Ip pulled his eyes in again and sank his head deep into his neck.

"You want some more cake, Becky?" I didn't wait for her to answer, but cut another slice and put it on her plate. Then I cut a slice for myself. It tasted so good. I ate and stared at Ip, hoping that my glaring would make him come out of hiding. I was almost finished with the whole piece before his blobby head pushed up again.

"I'll help you find the door to the spaceport," he said.

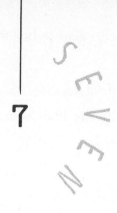

7

"SPACEPORT?" **I ASKED.** I turned to Becky. "*Spaceport!*"
I knew that space travel existed, separate from the passageway and the portals. But I had never *seen* a spaceship.

"There are many from species that don't live in the zoo," said Ip, rubbing his blobby hands together. "They trade with the Masters. The Brocine and the Hottini aren't like us — primitive species the Masters keep for entertainment. They're traders. The Brocine that poisoned your parent was kidnapped from a trade mission."

Ip glanced at Becky, who was stuffing the last of her second slice of cake into her face. "Helena must have wanted me to tell you if it sent that note."

"Tell us what?" My head was still spinning with the idea that the Brocine were kidnapped. Mom and Dad had always told me that the Masters *chose* people—

people who were glad to be lucky enough to live in the zoo.

Ip took a deep breath. "It's a secret." He blobbed over to me, making the floor squeak as he moved. His giant eyes bored into me. "You must never tell a Master. Never."

"I won't!" A secret from the Pipe Men? All of a sudden, it was hard to breathe. The Pipe Men knew everything. They were smarter than everyone in the universe. How could there be something they didn't know?

Ip sank his head into his neck a little, but then slowly let it pop out again. His horn vibrated as he spoke. "There is a network of Froms who live here in the zoo, people who want to plan how to escape. Some of us are miserable. Some, the Masters have kidnapped. The Hottini have agreed to help us because they want to undermine the Masters. When I met your parents, I told them about the plan. But they weren't interested. They wanted what the Masters offered."

"But they changed their minds?" I asked. It seemed impossible. They had never said anything like that to me. They had never even said a word against the Pipe Men. The Pipe Men really were Masters. We thanked them for everything we had.

Ip shook his horn. "Before now, no. They just wanted to be ready, to have a plan in case something changed."

"We could just leave, couldn't we?" I asked. It had never occurred to me before, but now that I thought about it, it seemed easy. We could just leave our house and go somewhere else on Earth. Or we could walk through Mom and Dad's closet and go into one of the portals.

Ip pressed his lips together, then released them with a pop. "We Froms only know what is behind the few doors the Masters show us. On Earth, there are more Masters and assistants than you know about. It's the same for all the zoo Froms. The plan is to escape to somewhere where the Masters are not in control." He paused.

"What are you talking about?" Becky said loudly. While I'd been listening to Ip, she'd gotten herself a third piece of cake. It looked like about half of it was on her face. Beneath the cake, she was glaring at me like she was about to pounce.

"He's telling me how we're getting to the spaceport," I said. I didn't think she'd run off and tell a Pipe Man about this secret escape plan, but I was just realizing something that I wasn't sure even I was ready to know. "Are you saying that Mom doesn't just want us to find a cure for Dad? Mom wants us all to leave the Masters forever? Leave O-thul-ba and Earth?"

"I don't know," said Ip. "For now, we'll get you to the spaceport. You bring back the cure. We'll deal then with what comes next."

I didn't know what to say, so I cut myself a third slice too. If *we bring back the cure*. If *we don't get caught doing it*.

Becky wiped her face with a napkin, but mostly only managed to spread the cake around. She was still glaring at me. But I couldn't figure out what to say to her.

Ip turned around so that his horn was facing us and slowly blobbed back into the living room.

"Wait!" I left the cake on the counter and ran after him. "What are you doing?"

Ip got down on his knees in front of the TV. His blobby legs smooshed grossly beneath him. He pushed the On button, then began sifting through the channels. "Why the numbering has to be different on every planet . . ." he muttered to himself.

As Ip sped through the channels, from after from appeared onscreen. We got TV from lots of planets, everywhere the Pipe Men wanted to connect us to. Some of the shows were fascinating and strange, and others were totally incomprehensible.

"Ah!" Ip said finally. "Here they are."

"Those are the Brocine?" I asked. The two Froms on the screen didn't look like rats. They looked more like giant dogs. They were standing in a pristine cabin, speaking in some unknown language. It sounded like barks and growls, yet the creatures delivered them standing very straight, as if orating Shakespeare. The picture was in black and white.

"No, these are the Hot*ti*ni," said Ip. "Emphasize the *ti*. The Brocine haven't come back to O-thul-ba since some of them were kidnapped, so they won't be at the spaceport. The Hottini can take you to the Brocine. And if all goes well, bring you back again. But we don't have much time. There's a Hottini ship leaving tonight, and it may be a week before another ship arrives."

"How do you know that?" I asked. The dog creatures — the Hottini — were still orating in their barks and growls. They were entirely covered in some kind of black material not unlike Pipe Man fabric, so all I could see was their heads and the vague outlines of their bodies.

I tried to get a closer look, but there wasn't much else to see.

Ip reached behind the TV with one arm and twisted something, then pulled a wire out and stuck it back in somewhere else. "The TVs work by tiny portals to the planet the transmission comes from. We use the portals to send messages."

"What?" Becky pulled up next to Ip on the floor and stared at the TV. "Doggies!" But her quick smile faded, and she looked up at me accusingly. "What's he doing?"

I quickly told her about the Hottini.

"Why can't we just find the Brocine through a portal?" Becky asked.

I was surprised I hadn't thought of it, so I translated for Ip.

"There are no permanent portals to any of the Brocine planets," he said. "If the Masters have ever opened one, I certainly don't know where it is." He smiled at Becky, his first smile since we'd read Mom's note. "That means we don't get their TV shows."

I translated for Becky.

"We're going on a spaceship!" said Becky, jumping up. "Vroom vroom!" She made her hand into a ship and whooshed it around in a circle.

At least Becky didn't seem scared. Then again, she probably didn't really understand what we were doing. I watched Becky whooshing around the living room. I had to believe I was doing the right thing. I was doing what Mom wanted us to do. But why hadn't she ever told me any of this herself?

I watched the screen. They seemed so distant and strange, and their speech was incomprehensible. "They do speak the Masters' language, don't they?"

"Yes, yes," said Ip. "As well as I do."

Becky gave her arm one last whoosh and sat down in front of the couch with a thump. "When are we going to see the puppies?"

"They're called Hot*ti*ni," I said. "Can you say that?"

"Hot*ti*ni," said Becky. "Would you like some soup?"

Ip burst out laughing, shaking the entire couch. "And what are puppies?" he asked Becky.

"They're like them," said Becky, pointing to the TV screen. "You throw them a ball and then they lick you."

"They're pets on Earth," I explained.

Ip shook his horn. "Becky, you can't treat the Hot*ti*ni like pets. You have to treat them the way you treat the Masters. Do you understand?"

I translated.

"Yes, they're going to take us on a spaceship, and we're going to get medicine for Dad, and the Pipe Men can't find out." Becky said it solemn-faced, oblivious to the cake still smeared over her cheek.

I translated.

"That's right," said Ip.

"Becky, why don't you wash that cake off your face?" I said.

She glared at me, but she walked into the kitchen.

I turned back to Ip, lowering my voice just in case Becky understood. "Is there anything else the Masters might do to us, besides making us stay on O-thul-ba? I mean, if we get caught."

Ip took a deep breath and leaned forward over his stomach, pointing his pomegranate eyes at mine. "I don't know if they'd hurt you. But if you have caused them enough trouble, they might sell you."

"Sell us?"

Ip took in my shocked expression. "Their access to exotic from species is one of the most prized assets of their control of the portals."

Sell us? How could they do that? Some of the Pipe Men were like family. I thought about Hon-tri-bum and all the other Pipe Man visitors, and Yel-to-tor and

Becky's tutor, Bre-zon-air. I couldn't believe they would do it. But what if they would? "But if we end up having to escape from the Masters, where are we supposed to go?" I asked.

Ip patted my head with a blobby arm, a bit too hard. "Don't worry. That's only the worst case. Maybe they won't even notice you're gone. You can come back, cure your parent, and nothing will change."

I nodded. I bet we were putting Ip and the other Froms in danger too. If I got caught, I'd put the whole escape route at risk for everyone else. I would just have to not get caught. We'd have to get the antidote and get back without the Pipe Men knowing about it.

8

I COULD HARDLY SLEEP THAT NIGHT. Dad would die unless I found the Brocine and got some kind of cure. But it didn't sound like it would be easy. And I had to take Becky with me. "Ryan and Becky," the note said. Why wouldn't she want Becky to be somewhere safe? Was she really just sending us away? Was she worried that the Pipe Men would hurt us? Would they cut us off from Earth like Ip had said? Sell us? And could these Hottini really help?

I woke up to Ip shaking me. His arm felt cold and slimy on my skin. My alarm clock said 3:26 a.m. I'd probably slept less than an hour.

"We have to go, Ryan. If we leave now, we might make it without the Masters seeing us."

Even though I hadn't slept much, I was wide awake. I jumped past Ip and put on the clothes I'd laid out for myself, the standard Pipe Man issued tunic and boots, with leggings to keep me from freezing. Then I picked up the backpacks I'd packed the night before. They had a change of clothes for me and Becky and a little bit of food and water. When I got to Becky's room, she was already awake and dressed in the same Pipe Man clothes as me.

"We're going through one of the doors!" she said, bouncing as I helped her slip on her backpack.

"Yeah, we'll get to see some more Froms," I said. Becky's cheerfulness was almost irritating. I was glad she didn't really understand what was going on, but having to act happy around her was already hard. She skipped ahead of me as we headed for Mom and Dad's bedroom.

Ip squeezed his way in front of me and into the closet. I felt the air suck away from me and knew he'd gone through the door. I'd always known that when you went through one of these doors, you went to another planet, and that that other planet might be so far away, you couldn't fly there in a spaceship in a million years. Somehow, the whole thing had never seemed strange before today. Today, I knew that there was a very real possibility that we might never be able to come back. Suddenly, I wondered about all the things outside our house on this side of the door. What would going to school be like now? What if I never had a single human friend? What if I never ate another peanut butter sandwich?

"Aren't we going?" Becky hopped up and down.

"Yeah, come on." I pushed her forward. It was too late for second thoughts. Mom had said to find the Brocine, and this was the only way to do it. I followed Becky through the door and into the passageway.

As we came out, Ip rolled his eyes back and forth and raised his arm over his mouth. I put my fingers to my lips, and Becky nodded. Ip folded his arms and globbed to our left, in the opposite direction from the door to the Pipe Man hospital. The passage was the same as before, all pinkish and soft with square, black, swirling doors. The doors went on down both sides of the passage as far as I could see.

I got as close to Ip as I could from behind, since it was impossible to stand next to him in the passageway. "How do you know which is the right door?" I whispered.

"The doors have numbers," he whispered back.

"Your closet is Z159. We're looking for 1064. So we have to count down to around 1064. But it also depends on bok."

"What's bok?" I asked.

"You haven't gotten to that yet?"

I shook my head.

"Urg . . . Well, it's not easy to explain. I don't really understand it. It's all about the way these portals work. Stuff nobody on Hdkowl knows anything about. It determines which portal goes to what."

That explanation hadn't helped me at all, but counting doors sounded simple enough. "So we just have to count down from Z159 to 1064."

Ip shook his head and rolled his eyes together. "No, when you deal with bok, it's not that simple. The doors change position. Even the Masters use a device called a calculator to get to the right place."

I thought about the rocklike device I'd seen the Pipe Men carrying. "Mom—Helena—didn't need a calculator to get to the hospital," I said.

"Most people can figure short distances," said Ip. "Some people even have a special talent. But not me."

"So you don't understand it, and you don't have this device?"

"We'll count until we get close. Odd numbers only. What do you have now?"

"What do I have?" I was so frustrated I almost shouted it, but managed to hold it to an angry whisper.

Ip shook soundlessly, like he was holding back a whole mountain full of laughter.

"It's not funny!" I whispered.

"I'm keeping count. This makes 2129." He stopped walking and stuck out a blobby arm, pointing at the door to our left. "You can count, too, if you don't trust me. Now be quiet. The later it gets, the more likely the Masters will come out."

"Count? What are we counting?" asked Becky.

"Doors. How many go by on one side."

"I want to count."

"Sure." It couldn't hurt. As long as Ip was right about the first thirty, which I wasn't at all sure of.

We started walking again, and this time I watched the doors as they went by. They were not solid black like a painted wall, but had different shades of black within them. Each one was a little different. They had patterns of shading inside them that moved and shifted. I knew there were planets behind each one of them. Other parts of O-thul-ba or new planets, places the Pipe Men would never let us see. I wanted to go through them, to see everything.

"My ears feel funny," Becky said.

Ip stopped suddenly. A Pipe Man came out of a door directly between him and us. Its eyes were facing Ip, not us. Ip turned to face it, arms raised high, then brought his arms down sharply in the ceremonial gesture.

"How are the Earth children withstanding?" asked the Pipe Man.

"Well, Tre-pet-on," said Ip. Ip flicked his horn sharply, as if trying to signal us.

I didn't know what Ip was trying to say, but I couldn't wait to find out. The Pipe Man could turn around at any second. I pulled Becky into the nearest door.

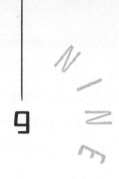

9

WE WERE IN A DARK PLACE. There was a little bit of light coming from somewhere far off, but at first, I couldn't see anything. The air was misty, and it was hot like a tropical island.

"Where are we?" Becky asked loudly.

"Shhh!" I clapped my hand over her mouth and stood as still as possible. Slowly, my eyes began to adjust. We were in some kind of cave. I saw part of a large boulder in the shadows, and the floor felt like smooth stone.

"Hello?" The voice was scratchy and deep.

I let out a breath and let go of Becky's mouth. If whatever was in here spoke Pipe Man, at least we had a chance to reason with it. "Hello," I said.

"Did you come through the door?"

"We seem to have taken a wrong turn," I said. I had to keep this From talking, make it let us stay here. I couldn't be sure the Pipe Man would be gone yet. I still couldn't see the From in the dim light.

"Earth people!" the voice said.

"Yes! How do you know that?"

A head began emerging out of the darkness. It had two large antennae growing out of its forehead, with nothing recognizable as eyes. A mouth in the middle of its face opened in what I hoped was a smile. At least there weren't any sharp teeth. "From the Masters," said the creature. "I've been learning all the From species. Earth people. Arms and legs!"

"I've never heard of you!" said Becky. She pulled forward, still holding my hand, and reached out to the creature. "What are you?"

I wanted to pull her back, but I didn't want to offend it. Now that it had seen us, we needed it to be our friend.

"I'm a Frontringhor person. This is my planet."

"How . . . old are you?" Becky labored out the Pipe Man words.

"Becky, that's not polite."

"It's fine," said the creature. "I would be happy to answer if I knew. I have simply been here a long time."

It took me a second to realize what it had just said. "You speak English?"

"I speak all languages."

"How?" I asked.

"A kind of telepathy. I didn't know I could do it until the Pipe Men came."

"That's amazing. I'm Ryan, and this is my sister Becky. I'm sorry we dropped in on you like this."

"Oh, no," said the creature. "It's my pleasure. I don't often get visitors. Other than the Pipe Men, of course."

"Do you have a zoo sector too?" asked Becky.

"Oh, yes," said the creature. "A rubbery, poor imitation of Frontringhor, I'm afraid." The tone could have been bitter, but I wasn't sure.

"Do you ever get to go into the passage?" Becky asked.

The creature pulled forward toward us, revealing a short, thin neck, followed by an eel-like body, which grew gradually bigger around. The end of it remained in darkness. The head pulled forward toward the door, sticking its antennae out so that they almost touched the blackness. Its smile twisted. "I would like to visit other places," it said.

"Why don't you?" Becky asked.

"The Pipe Men won't let me, Becky. You see, I am the only one of my kind. They do not want to risk losing me."

"But if you're the only one, then who do you talk to?" I asked.

"I talk to the Pipe Men who come see me. Occasionally, other Froms visit my sector." It lifted its antennae until they were at the same level as my eyes. "I would like to talk to others. It is a curse, to know I can talk to anyone in any language, but to be stuck here."

"We'll talk to you," said Becky. "Now that we know you're here, we'll come back."

The creature slid its antennae partway back down, until they were on Becky's level. "Thank you, Becky. That is very nice of you. I hope you will truly do it."

"What's your name?" she asked.

"I don't have a name," it said. "I'm just the From from Frontringhor."

"We could call you Mr. Frontringhor," said Becky.

"Or just Front," I said.

"Call me what you want," said the creature. "But tell

me why you've come here. I know the Pipe Men do not let the Earth children walk around."

"We're hiding," I said. "It's a long story. But we have to get somewhere without the Pipe Men knowing."

"I suspected as much." The creature pulled its antennae back to what I assumed was their normal level. "Well, I won't give you away. The Pipe Men are my jailers, not my friends."

Before today, I had never thought about the fact that we really were captives, or wondered how the other Froms in the zoo felt about it. The zoo on O-thʊl-ba was still more my home than Earth was. What if I never got to see it again? That would be worse for me than being cut off from Earth. I forced myself to focus. One thing was clear. Front felt trapped, and he might be able to help us. I suddenly got an idea. "Do you understand bok?"

The creature smiled. "I understand it."

"Can you help us? We have to find the right door." I wasn't going to let on to Becky, but I wasn't sure that Ip could really get us where we were going. *If* he was even still in the passage. That Pipe Man could have taken him away, or scared him enough so that he ran off on his own. I just hoped he wasn't getting punished because of us.

"Follow me," said Front. He pulled his head backward and disappeared into the darkness.

I took a deep breath and looked at Becky. She smiled widely. To her, this whole thing was probably one big adventure. I gripped her hand tighter and took a step. As I moved, I could see a little farther. The light was increasing, slowly but surely.

"I hope the light makes it easier for you," Front said from the darkness.

I took another step, and the cave began to really brighten. There were more boulders and, between them, Front's body, which extended back into the distance, all the way out of the cave and into the landscape. As it extended, it grew to at least five feet wide, so big that I couldn't have reached my arms across Front's back. I couldn't see the end of him.

"Another obstacle to me leaving," said Front, "as you can see."

10

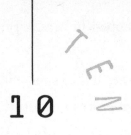

I HELD ON TO BECKY'S HAND and led her between the boulders. The closer we got to the cave entrance, the more I could feel a strong, wet breeze. The brightness around us seemed to be coming from everywhere at once, but I didn't see any source for it. Outside, the Frontringhor landscape was still shrouded in semidarkness. Front's head was waiting for us at the entrance, but I still couldn't see the end of him.

"I know your eyes will not be able to see far, but my home is really a very beautiful planet."

There was just enough light coming from the cave, and from some faint glow far off in the distance, for me to see that the landscape was made up of short hills covered by low vegetation. There were pockets of shininess that might have been ponds or bogs. I wondered if

I would sink up to my knees when I stepped out of the cave.

"Is it solid?" I asked.

"If you stay behind my body, I will lead you over safe ground." Front slowly slid backward, leaving a path for us to walk on.

"Are there any animals?" asked Becky.

"I have never seen any," said Front.

"Then what do you eat?"

"How did you evolve?" I asked at the same time.

Front smiled his toothless smile. "I do not eat as you do. What I need is in the air and the water and the land. My planet and I are tied together, like two parts of one being."

"Does that mean it would hurt to leave?" asked Becky.

Front closed his mouth so that he was no longer smiling. "Yes. But not nearly as much as it hurts to stay."

"Do the Pipe Men hurt you?" she asked.

Front didn't answer. We walked in silence for a minute.

"We're not supposed to go out," said Becky, "but I don't want to. Earth people are mean."

"You don't seem mean to me," said Front, smiling again.

"We're not! We're better than regular Earth people."

It disturbed me that Becky said that, but I wasn't sure why. That was what both the Pipe Men and our parents had taught us, that we were better than other Earth people because the Pipe Men had chosen us. That we were smarter because we learned from the Pipe Men. But the Pipe Men could have come through any other closet. Was there really something different about us?

"The Pipe Men said that to me, too," said Front. "A long time ago, when they first came."

"What did they say?" I asked.

"They said that I was better than the other Frontringhor people because they had chosen me. When I told them that I was the only one, they told me that I was better than all the others in the universe that they had not chosen."

"Do you think it's true?" I asked.

"I don't know, Ryan. I have never met a Froм they have not chosen."

The ground beneath our feet was squooshy, but not in the same way as O-thυl-ƀɑ. The ground on O-thυl-

ᚦᚨ was artificial, created out of their rubbery fabric for reasons only the Pipe Men knew. The Frontringhor ground was soft because it was saturated with water, growing with life. My Id-won hide boots had never walked on natural ground before. In the distance we walked, the landscape in front of us did not change. I glanced behind us and saw the cave we had come from, embedded in a hill that, once we were away from it, did not seem much larger than the others. Only the light still coming from the cave mouth made it stand out.

"Where are we going?" I asked.

"To get something you need. We are here."

We were at another cave entrance. It was not big enough for us to walk into, since the thickest part of Front's body was already in it. Without another word, Front rolled his head over the top of his body, back into the blackness. I hesitated for a second, trying to see into the darkness. Then a faint glow began to build. What I saw made me jump and pull Becky backward.

She shrieked in surprise.

Front's head was no longer visible. It had folded back over itself like a bent hot dog. The beginning of the body also disappeared into the darkness of the cave, and the body rolled over itself so that another part of the body came into view from underneath. Front's body rolled and rolled for what seemed like several minutes. Then his head suddenly appeared again, rolling up off the ground. The head slid toward us, letting the last revolution of the body slowly fade away into the darkened cave. His mouth was full of something, and he thrust it toward me.

I recognized it as the device the Pipe Men had been carrying when they'd led us back to Earth—the calculator Ip had mentioned. I reached out for it and took it from the creature's mouth, trying not to notice the slight coating of saliva. The device was oddly shaped, made of some kind of synthetic material. It was small enough to hold in one hand, but its edges were jagged, as if it had been dropped and broken. It was the color of stone, and it didn't appear to have any buttons or screen at all.

"I'm sorry if I scared you," said Front, turning his antennae to Becky. "I suppose I seem very strange to you."

"How did you do that?" Becky leaned forward, trying see over Front's body and into the cave. Just at the edge of the darkness was the outline of more of Front's body, coiled and piled on itself.

"It comes naturally to me."

"Where did you get this?" I asked.

"From my sector," said Front. He stretched his head forward, elongating his neck, stretching it out two feet, then three. "My body can't go through the door, but my head can make it to the glass." Front smiled sadly as he let his head drop gently back.

"This is a calculator?"

"Push there." Front moved one of his antennae to point at a jagged piece of material sticking out of the device's side.

I pushed it. It was soft under my finger. The top of the calculator began to glow. "Now what am I supposed to do with it?"

"You have learned nothing about bok?"

I shook my head.

"Bok is how the Pipe Men are able to use the portals. Before they understood bok, they had to travel in spaceships, spending years in travel, never reaching anywhere. When they discovered bok, all that changed." The tinge of bitterness edged Front's voice again.

"But what is it?"

"It is a great deal more than even the Pipe Men know. At the basic level they understand, it is the sum of the uncertainties of the final variables of each integer."

"I don't exactly understand final variables yet." I frowned down at the device. I knew what Yel-to-tor would say. I should have been able to understand this.

"Ryan's not good at math," said Becky, giggling.

"For example," said Front, "when you count to one hundred, bok gives you the chance that you'll actually arrive there."

"How could I not arrive there?"

"Often."

The calculator glowed at me, mocking me for my ignorance. "Look, I'm not going to learn this right now. Can you just show me how to use this thing to find the right door?"

Front reached an antenna toward me so that it hovered over the calculator in my hand. I suddenly noticed that there were still two antennae sitting back near Front's head. "You have three?"

"This head does."

"Two heads! Ohmigosh! Are there more?" Becky

leaned even farther into the cave, so that she was nearly climbing on Front's back.

"Becky, don't go poking around!"

Front's second head smiled. "No, Becky, there are only two. One for each end."

"I wish I had two heads." Becky came back toward us and patted Front just behind the head we saw.

I held my breath, not sure if Front would be angry, but he merely pointed his first two antennae at her and continued smiling. His third antenna pressed the calculator where it was glowing. Suddenly, a screen appeared, which was divided into a grid.

"The Pipe Men have named many of the doors in the passage with numbers. What door number are you looking for?"

"1064," I said.

Front's third antenna turned away from the screen and rose to the level of my face. "Why are you going to 1064?"

"We're trying to get to some spaceport," I said. "On another part of O-thul-ba, outside the zoo."

"Outside the zoo." Front's antennae hovered. "You want to meet the Hottini."

"How did you know that?" I gasped.

"I'm sorry," said Front. "I didn't mean to read your mind."

"What am I thinking?" Becky wrapped her arm around Front's neck and put her face right in front of his.

"Becky, stop it! We have to find this door!"

Becky sat down on the ground and folded her arms.

I sighed. "I'm sorry. Yes, the Hottini will be at the spaceport. We just have to find this door."

"The door you are at is number 44. When you go out, touch 44," said Front.

"44?" I asked. "But we were going from 2159 to 1064!"

"Often the doors remain in order," said Front. "But often they do not."

I sighed again. This was making my brain hurt. Where the screen had before been a blank grid, it was now filled with numbers in the Pipe Man script.

"Then touch the number you want to get to, in this case, 1064. You can get to more numbers by rolling your finger along here." Front touched his antenna to a series of small jagged points on top of the device. "It will take you along a path. You will see."

"What if I don't understand it? Can't I try it out somehow?"

"It will be clear. Just make sure you check the door number before you go through it. They can change moment by moment."

"The one that goes from our sector to our house doesn't change," Becky said.

"Becky—" I shut my mouth. She was right. Wasn't she?

Front lowered one of his antennae to her eye level. "The Pipe Men use a version of this technology to create portals that stay the same and that exist outside the passage." He tapped the calculator with his first antenna. "They can make portals of any size if they have enough raw materials." Front was no longer smiling.

"That makes you sad," said Becky.

Front smiled again. "But you make me happy." He turned two of his antennae to me. "Listen to your sister, Ryan. She has a natural talent."

Becky giggled and jumped to her feet. "I have a natural talent!"

"Okay." So she noticed things sometimes. I still wasn't at all sure that it would be as easy as Front made it sound.

"Do not let the Pipe Men catch you with this," said Front. "If they do catch you, it did not come from me."

"Of course not. Thank you so much, Front. I wish you could come with us."

"Perhaps in time."

"We'll come back and visit you."

"I would like that very much." Front smiled wide, opening his mouth several inches. I was glad it was too dark to see inside. He pointed all three antennae at Becky. "You will visit, too, won't you?"

"Of course!" She threw her arms around the creature's neck.

We started walking, staying next to Front, careful not to step out into the bog. Becky kept her hand on Front's back, and he didn't seem to mind. It was not long before we were in the first cave, standing before the black door, which I now knew was number 44.

"Goodbye, Front," I said.

"Goodbye, Ryan, Becky. I will see you again soon."

"Goodbye!" Becky hugged the giant alien again, and again, he smiled wide. It was only after I pushed Becky before me and took a glance back toward him that I saw his smile fade and his antennae, all three of them, droop down over his face.

11

THERE WAS NO ONE in the passageway. I wondered where Ip was, but I didn't have time to worry about it. We had to get to the door before anyone saw us.

Becky pulled my arm like she wanted to go.

"Wait," I whispered. "We have to do this here." I looked down at the calculator. The screen was still glowing. The numbers did not appear to be exactly in order, but 44 was easy to pick out. I touched it with my finger; 44 blinked and then the numbers on the grid changed. I saw numbers in the hundreds, but 1064 was not on there. I scrolled like Front had shown me, and there it was. I pressed it.

The screen changed from the grid filled with numbers to something else. There were lines going in all directions, nothing that seemed to resemble the passage I was standing in.

"Let me see," said Becky.

"Shhh," I whispered, but I showed it to her.

"Here," she said. She pointed toward the far right side of the screen.

As I followed her finger, it suddenly clicked. Door 44 was at the bottom right-hand corner, and the passage went diagonally up the screen, toward the upper left-hand corner. The lines marking the passage were not solid, but were broken by gaps of different lengths. Other lines shot off in all directions and filled the screen in a seemingly random pattern, but a passage-shaped space remained in the middle, thicker in some places and thinner in others. I looked around at the doors, as if they might have moved and become irregular like the picture in front of me, but they looked the same as always. Large, black, rectangular gaps in space.

A chill went through my body. I had never thought about how any of this worked before. I had just walked through a closet and been on O-thʋl-þᴙ. It had been as normal to me as walking from one room to another in my house. But this was not normal. There was more here than I'd ever imagined.

I started walking in the direction we'd been going before the Pipe Man had appeared. As I advanced, a tiny line appeared on the screen, moving with me.

"Come on," I whispered. "We have to move quickly." Whether we were still near 44 or back between 2159 and 1064, we had a ways to go, so I set off at a brisk pace, almost running. At the same time, I tried to think of an excuse, a reason why we might be here, in case a Pipe Man came through one of the doors again. I decided to say that we were looking for the hospital, that we'd purposely ditched Ip so we could see our parents. It seemed reasonable. They'd just send us back to the zoo and have some Pipe Men watch over us. They'd have no reason to suspect we were trying to escape.

The thought almost made me stop walking. *Were* we trying to escape? Was that really what Mom wanted? Or did she just want us to find the antidote and come back? She'd said to go with Ip, and Ip said we might have to escape. But if we escaped, we somehow had to get the antidote to Dad first. And speaking of Ip, where *was* he?

I checked my place on the screen. I couldn't tell what

number we were at. It just showed the line moving along with us. On the screen, the path appeared straight, but in front of me, the passage began curving sharply.

"Was this passage curving a minute ago?" I whispered.

Becky shook her head and took a step closer to me. "My ears." She rubbed both of them with her hands.

"It's okay. Things are different here. We're in . . ." I trailed off, not sure how to describe it. I didn't really know myself. "A place where things are different." I kept walking at the slower pace. Becky stayed right with me. Soon we passed around the sharp curve, which seemed to become sharper even as we walked around it.

There was Ip, standing in the passage, facing us. He threw up his arms, almost like he would for the ritual greeting. "Ryan and Becky! You are all right!" Ip moved forward quickly, arms outstretched as if to hug us. I braced for the impact of his blobby arms, but he stopped suddenly before he reached us.

"Ip!" cried Becky, and she hugged him herself, throwing her arms around his monstrous middle.

"Where did you get that?" Ip was looking down at the calculator in my hand.

"We don't have time to talk about it," I whispered. A tiny light was blinking on the screen. "It says we're close to 1064."

"We should be. I've been waiting here since I lost you — and put off that Master. This is the one by my count." Ip pointed his horn to the door on my left, just in front of me.

"It says it's this one." I pointed to the door on the right, across the passage from Ip's suggestion.

Ip leaned over me and peered at the calculator. "So it does. But Ryan, who gave this to you? The Masters will find out it's missing. They don't let Froms keep them."

I hadn't had time to worry about that. What would the Pipe Men do to Front if they found out he'd taken it? My mind filled with his drooping antennae. I wasn't sure it was safe even to tell Ip.

"It was Front," said Becky. "It's big and . . . long . . . with two . . . heads and . . ." Becky's Pipe Man failed her.

"Big with two heads? There's only one From I know of like that. The Frontringhor. Ryan, was that the door you went through?" Ip was no longer looking at the calculator. He stared at me with wide red eyes.

"It gave me this. It seemed lonely. Happy to see us.

And upset enough with the Masters to help us. We told it we were going to the spaceport, but it helped anyway."

"You told it?" Ip's eyes seemed to grow even bigger, and his mouth twisted into an expression I'd never seen. "Let's get out of this passage." Ip turned around so quickly that his horn almost knocked into my face. He globbed through the door the calculator had picked, the one that was now blinking on the screen with the number 1064.

"Is he all right?" Becky asked.

"Yes, we just need to keep moving." I grabbed her hand and went to follow Ip, but then I noticed something blinking on the screen. I had to look at it again to be sure I really saw it: 1064 was no longer where it had been. According to the calculator, 1064 was now the one on the left, the one Ip had picked out.

"Why aren't we going?" Becky tugged on my tunic with one hand and rubbed her ear with the other.

"We . . . it says it's that one now." I rubbed my eyes and looked again. It still said that door 1064 was on the left.

"That's how it works," said Becky. "Remember? 'They can change moment by moment.'" Becky's imitation of

Front's gruff voice was so good I almost laughed. But I wanted to cry.

"But Ip went that way," I said.

She paused for a second, her hand over her ear. "Then let's get him and come back."

What Becky said made sense. I took a deep breath. "Okay. We'll get him and come back." Still holding Becky's hand, I stepped through the door we'd just seen Ip go through. Suddenly I was choking. Dust swirled around me, and there was a brightness that blinded me even more. I couldn't see anything. I couldn't breathe. Becky was coughing, her hand gripping mine like a vise. I stepped backward, praying the door would be there. We were back in the passage. I dropped to my knees, gasping.

"Where did you go? I leave you for ten seconds!" Ip was behind me, pounding on my back as I coughed up maroon-colored dust.

"We thought you were there," I choked. "We wanted to tell you it was the wrong door. It was — " I started coughing again.

"You've got water in that backpack."

I realized he was right and twisted my arms out of the backpack. I pulled out a bottle and unscrewed the top, then handed it to Becky. She coughed for a few more seconds, then took it and drank. After I also drank some, I finally started to really breathe again. Then I heard the voices.

"Presumptively ready, though the absence of Froms will leave us with some work to do," said a Pipe Man.

"A useful place eventually," said another.

I had set the calculator on the ground during my coughing fit, and it was covered in dust. Ip picked it up, stared at it, then rubbed his giant arm over the calculator screen.

I took it from him. "This one again," I whispered. I pointed to the one we had just come from, the one that had made us choke. I didn't have time to contemplate this, because Ip got behind both Becky and me and pushed. I barely had time to grab my backpack before I was falling through the door.

12

WE WERE OBVIOUSLY IN the spaceport. Behind us, a wall rose many eyes over our heads, but in front of us, it was all open. Giant spacecraft sat at irregular intervals out into the distance. The floor was illuminated, but through the light, I could see up to the night sky. A small gap in the cloud cover revealed a patch of stars.

"Where's Ip?" Becky asked.

"Shhh!" I pulled her close to me. Ip hadn't come through behind us, which meant that he was talking to the Pipe Men. Had they seen us leaving? Was Ip in trouble? I tried to steady my breathing, to not show Becky that I was scared, and to look around calmly.

People moved quickly about the floor. There were all kinds of people, all shapes and sizes of Froms. I thought

I recognized some of them from TV, but I couldn't be sure. Several creatures about Becky's size with fat, featherless wings and three tall, spindly legs each tripped by us, so lightly that they made no noise. Another creature with a tiny head and four giant metallic feet tromped across the floor so loudly that I wanted to cover my ears, even though it was ten yards away.

None of the Froms paid any attention to us.

The only Pipe Men I saw were two tall ones standing next to the entrance to a small building that sat on the left edge of the floor. They were wearing some kind of covering over their top-holes, and I couldn't tell if any of their eyes were looking at us.

I pushed Becky to our right, so we could get a little farther away from the Pipe Men. Suddenly, a loud buzzing started all around us.

"Clear. Clear. Clear," said a loud, calm voice.

I pulled Becky toward me.

Some of the Froms who had been scurrying around the spacecraft headed toward the building where the Pipe Men stood. The three-legged bird things headed toward us. I hoped that meant we were safe here. The birds backed up against the wall, and I pulled Becky up against it too. We were right next to a different kind of From, with six thin legs and a fat body with three distinct sections, each one a little smaller than the one below it. Three horizontally arranged eyes examined us.

"Pleasant day," I said.

The spidery From blinked its three eyes and rubbed its legs together, making a humming sound.

"I don't understand," I said.

"It doesn't have a mouth," said Becky.

I quickly realized that she was right, and wondered if it even could hear me. It didn't have anything that looked like ears. But a loud noise stopped me from thinking about it.

The ship was one of the smallest I saw, but it was still as big as half of our house. It was shaped like a lemon, standing up on one impossibly small end. Now it was emitting loud bursts of noise, like radio static amplified many times over. Smoke or steam was coming from near the bottom of the lemon tip. Suddenly it fell away from us, stopping so that its body was horizontal, suspended in midair only a few eyes off the ground. The smoke began swirling all around it, and then there was one long, louder burst of static, and the ship rose up into the air, straight up and up and up until I couldn't see it anymore.

"Clear," said the calm voice.

The Froms around us hurried off in all directions, all except for the spiderlike one with the three eyes and no mouth, who stared at us, unmoving.

"Can you understand me?" I asked.

The From began shaking, the three sections of its body slowly waving.

I pulled Becky backward and looked around me. Where could we run to? But then I realized what the From was doing.

It was shaking off a thin cloak, which I had assumed was part of the creature's skin. It lifted one leg and pulled the cloak all the way off, then stuck another leg into a pocket and pulled out a tablet. I quickly recognized it as the kind our Pipe Men tutors used. The From began typing on the keypad with two legs. After a minute, it held out the tablet to me.

I took it.

I can hear you, it said.

As I read, the From pointed with one leg to a spot in the middle section of its body. Most of the body was a deep and dirty brown color, but this spot was much lighter, almost a perfect rectangle.

Becky reached out her hand, trying to touch it.

"Becky!"

The From blinked at her.

I went on reading. I saw you come out of the portal. I have never seen your species here before. Are you in trouble with the Masters?

"What does it say?" asked Becky.

"It saw us come out." The fact that this From was still standing here instead of tattling on us to the Pipe Men had to mean something. I decided to take a leap of faith. "Yes, we are. We need to get to the Hottini ship. Can you help us?"

The From lifted the tablet from my hands. Its legs were so thin and light, it was amazing that they could hold the tablet's weight, much less support the creature's body. Quickly, it typed again.

Yes. You must get out of the open before they see you. Follow me.

"It wants us to follow it," I said to Becky. "What do you think?"

"He's nice," she said. She smiled at the creature and reached out a hand again.

The creature lifted a leg and very lightly touched her finger. To me, it seemed like its eyes were smiling. I knew that this was the most reassurance I was likely to get.

"Okay, lead the way."

Its eyes twitched, viewing the floor of the space dock. The two Pipe Men were no longer in sight, and no one else seemed to be watching us. It walked quickly to our right, away from the Pipe Men, along the side of the wall, so lightly that its legs barely touched the ground.

We followed until it reached the end of the wall. From there, I could see a few spaceships before the lit area ended. After that, the city lights twinkled in the darkness. Pipe Man buildings were tall and thin like the Pipe Men themselves, and they went up hundreds of eyes into the sky. Between the buildings, assistant wires let off bursts of light as they transferred power, food, and anything else the Pipe Men needed. It struck me that there were no assistant wires out here in the space dock. That made me breathe easier. The Pipe Men never went anywhere without assistants, and if they were using a transport assistant — like an Earth car — at least I'd be able to see them coming.

We set off across the floor and passed the first

spaceship. This one was larger than the one we'd just seen take off. It was a perfect sphere, surrounded by short, squat Froms with leathery green skin and one thick leg each. They moved by standing on their toes, using them like mini-legs. In their four arms they held various tools and were busy hammering and tugging at the ship's hull. A few of them turned to look as we passed by, pointing their single eyes at us, but none of them made any move in our direction.

"They're on TV," said Becky.

She was right. I remembered their channel. There were no Pipe Men subtitles, but there was a lot of eating what appeared to be raw animal flesh with large, sharp teeth. I hurried to catch up with our new friend, who was now walking faster and faster, heading for the next ship.

The ship sat high above us, on a single long pole that ended on the spaceport floor with a platform shaped like a hand with six equidistant, spindly claws. As we watched, a hatch opened in the hull. Several more Froms just like our friend jumped out of it. The door had to be at least seventy eyes up in the air, but the Froms landed softly next to their comrade. They looked so much alike,

I couldn't tell which one was which, until the one who had been leading us stepped back out of the group and waved a leg.

Becky and I hurried forward.

"Hello! I'm Becky!" Becky said loudly, pointing at her chest.

Several sets of three eyes blinked at us.

"I'm Ryan," I said, not sure what else to do.

Our friend reached out three of its legs, and another one stepped forward and did the same. They wrapped their legs together, making a net. Then our friend reached up another leg and waved to us, pointing at their locked legs.

"It wants us to get on," said Becky.

Our friend waved at us again, then pointed to the open hatch.

"It's so far," I said. "How are they going to get us up there? How are you going to get us up there?"

Our friend pointed to one of the others. The second one jumped, and with one push of its six spindly legs, it landed back inside the ship. It turned and waved three legs at us.

"See?" said Becky. "They can jump high."

And we would never be able to get down without their help. "Can you just tell us how to get to the Hottini ship? We don't want to cause you trouble."

Our friend blinked at us and pointed again at the hammock they had made of legs.

I looked around us. For all I knew, we might be at the wrong end of the space dock, and there were ships everywhere, all manned by different Froms. They might not be as friendly as these people. And those two Pipe Men with their weird top-hole coverings were back. Was it my imagination, or were they looking our way?

"Okay," I said to Becky. "Listen to me. We can never get separated. You can never go more than a foot away from me. I don't care what happens. Do you understand me?"

Becky nodded.

"Okay." I took her hand, and we moved toward the outstretched legs. The Froms bent the legs they were standing on so that their hammock was low to the ground. We lay down on it, and I pulled Becky close to me. Their legs wrapped around us, encircling our bodies. It was hard to remain calm. Then we were airborne.

13

WE LANDED SO QUICKLY and softly that I didn't have a chance to panic. The legs slowly unwrapped from around us, and I stumbled to my feet. Then I panicked. I was at the edge of the ship's cargo hold, staring down at the ground, which was way too far below me. I stepped backward and tripped over Becky, knocking us both to the floor.

"I'm sorry! Are you all right? I . . ." I couldn't finish my sentence. Now I was staring up at the insides of the spaceship. There were three balconies above us, winding their way around the open bay. Each balcony was filled with identical buglike Froms. There were so many of them that their legs seemed to thread together in a mass, and their eyes all stared down at us.

Suddenly, the hatch we'd just come through slammed

shut. I sat up and reached for Becky, but my hand hit the cold floor. Then one of the Froms was on top of me. Its body was hot and rancid, and its legs wrapped around me, digging into my arms and back. I tried to turn my head, to get my nose away from the stink, but one of its legs was pressing my head into its belly. I tried to call out for Becky, but instead, my mouth caught in its coarse, wet hair.

I spit and tried to scream, but there was more hair, and its legs pressed my face so close that I couldn't move my mouth at all and I couldn't see anything. My back lifted completely off the floor, into the air. We landed on a balcony, and then we were moving at a run. Spindly legs brushed against my shoulders. My backpack bounced against the floor, pressing my face even farther into the creature's hair. I could feel more of them around me. The air was moister with them all around, clamming up my exposed hands. The From ran smoothly, making it hard to tell how far we'd gone.

I kept hearing humming around me. It was an awful sound, whiny and sour, just as bad on the ears as the thing's belly was on my nose. I tried to kick, but it held me so tight, there wasn't any room for me to move my legs. I managed to twist my face sideways, so I could take a deep breath through my nose. With one eye, I saw the legs flying by me, the lower bodies of the Froms that were now looking even more like insects. My view changed to empty space. I felt sick to my stomach and closed my eyes, still trying to take a deep breath.

Then I was suddenly free, kicking and flailing my arms, sucking in air. I kicked something hard and with a curse, opened my eyes. I was staring up from the bottom of a pit. Some thirty eyes up, six insect eyes stared back at me.

"Becky!"

They were rubbing their legs together up there, and the awful humming noise was coming out.

"Becky!"

"Ryan!"

"Becky! Where are you?"

"I'm in a pit somewhere! I don't know!"

"Are you hurt?"

"No. What happened? Why don't they like us?"

"I don't know. Don't worry! I'll find a way to get us out of this!" I sat up in my pit. I found that I wasn't really hurt. The tightness of the creature's grip had kept me from knocking around too much. There were only a few places where the legs had cut into my skin. "Hey, you!" I called up to them. "Why did you do this? Why do you want us?"

The Froms hummed at each other. I wanted to cover my ears, but I didn't want them to see that it bothered me.

"Well?" I shouted. "We didn't do anything to you!"

One of them landed in front of me, having jumped so quickly that I hadn't even seen it. Without meaning to, I gasped and pressed my back against the wall. Then it reached one of its legs around and came back with the tablet, typing quickly.

You are not from the space flight systems. You have escaped from the Masters' zoo.

My heart sank. "You can't take us back! Please, they'll . . . I don't know what they'll do. I have to find the Hottini. You can't take us back!"

We are not taking you back. You are worth a great deal on the market.

"On the market? What market?" But I remembered what Ip had said. Why hadn't I remembered it sooner?

Exotic creatures from planets only reached by portal. Very expensive to buy from the Masters. All three of its eyes examined me. It took the tablet back with two legs and stared at me a second longer. Then it jumped, and both it and its friend were gone.

"What did it tell you?" came Becky's voice.

I sighed and leaned back against the smooth metal wall of the pit, closing my eyes. "They're going to sell us. Zoo people are worth a lot of money."

"I thought it was nice." I heard sobs in her voice.

"I did too," I said. "I should have realized how much we'd stick out. I'm sorry, Becky. It's my fault." How could I have gotten her into this?

All I heard was her sobbing.

"Look, I'm going to get us out of this. I just . . ." I stared up and around me. The walls of the pit were perfectly smooth. There was nothing to grab on to at all. I ran my hand along the wall. It was faintly warm. "I just wish I could jump up thirty eyes," I said, too softly for Becky to hear.

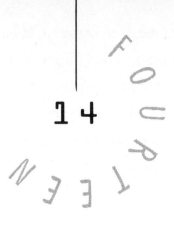

14

I SMASHED AGAINST THE WALL of the pit, then rolled along the bottom. I tried to stop myself, but there was nothing to hold on to. "I think we're moving!" I called. But we couldn't be taking off. We'd never get back to O-thʊl-ba. I'd never see my parents again. Dad would die.

The ship gave another roll. This wasn't how the ship I'd seen before had taken off. It had risen gracefully into the sky. Something had to be wrong. Then we were tipping. I was rolling toward the top of the pit!

"Becky! Roll out of the pit! Roll out now!" We were stable for a second. Horizontal. I crawled along the wall that was now the floor. I went as fast as I could, but it was slippery. I tried pushing myself and sliding. "Slide!" I cried. "Becky, can you hear me? Slide!" I was making progress now, almost to the edge. Then the ship tipped ever so slightly, and I started slipping back. I clawed at the walls, but it didn't do any good. I kept slipping.

"Ryan!" Becky appeared at the top of the pit, hanging on to the edge.

"Stay there! Don't let go!"

"I'm trying!"

I reached out both arms and legs and jammed them against the sides, stopping myself. With all my limbs outstretched, I could just barely hold on. But I knew I couldn't do it for long. My arms were already aching, and the ship kept tilting slowly backward. It was like they'd gotten control again, and the walls were just too slippery. I pressed as hard as I could, but I couldn't hold myself in place.

Suddenly, the ship rolled forward. I fell out of the pit headfirst, flying past Becky. She was struggling to hold on to the thin barrier between what I now saw were two of several pits with openings in a row across the floor. Things were rolling out of the other pits, round and square items wrapped in Pipe Man fabric. One knocked into me. I braced myself to fall more but realized that I was not moving. I was floating. Weightless.

Becky was still trying to hang on to the edge of the pits, but her legs were now kicking up in the air.

"Just let go!" I called.

"We're going to fall again!"

I knew she was probably right. I didn't think we were supposed to be weightless. "Just let go, and we'll get out of this room, so we can't fall into the pits."

She let go and floated upward toward me, kicking, trying to right herself.

The ship was not completely right side up again, but it was getting closer. I saw only one exit, but through it, I also saw the many legs of weightless Froms. They were kicking around wildly, as if they were just as unprepared for this as we were. A terrible screeching noise was coming from their legs.

I caught Becky's arm and helped twist her so we were both upright relative to the floor and the pits below. "I think we should go now. They can't run while they're weightless. We'll push off against the walls."

"What if they catch us?" One of her tears floated up into the air.

I held on to her hand. "They're not going to hurt us. We're worth a lot of money. Okay?"

She nodded.

I knew we didn't have time to waste. By kicking out one of my legs, I could just reach a wall. I pushed. Slowly, we floated toward the opposite wall. "Okay, push that way," I said, pointing back into the room. "We'll end up going the other way, toward the exit."

Becky nodded.

We both pushed, and it worked. One more push, and we were through the door. It was chaos. The noise was deafening. The bug Froms were crashing into each other, flying in all directions. As we came out, several looked at us. They jostled against each other, trying to propel in our direction.

I pushed as hard as I could against the doorway, trying to send us down the wall, but instead we floated toward the edge of the balcony and the mass of swarming Froms. A few more seconds and we'd be over the giant open bay, many long levels below us. I grabbed the railing that separated the balcony from the bay and held on. Becky had the balcony in one hand and my hand in the other. The creatures were all around us, humming.

All at once, the humming got even louder. Air whooshed around me, as if the Froms were crashing even more violently against each other. Over it all, I heard a clomping sound, like a giant was plodding slowly down the passage.

"It's a doggie!" said Becky.

I followed where she was looking. It was twice as big as I was and walked on four legs. On each foot it wore a large, heavy boot that seemed to take quite a bit of effort to lift and move. The boots must have been holding the creature down, because it labored slowly along the balcony toward us, unaffected by the weightlessness. On top of the four legs was a doglike body, long and thick and muscled, layered with a see-through covering like a rain poncho. Its head was wide and sat on a long neck, but it had only two lidless eyes, a thin nose, and a mouth at the bottom of its face. Its whole body was covered in something like hair, but the strands were much thicker than any hair I'd ever seen. It almost looked like Pipe Man fabric that had been dyed a deep blue and cut into strips. The strange blue hair flapped calmly as the Hottini kept walking toward us.

"Don't call it a doggie," I whispered. "Remember what Ip told us."

The Hottini reached us and stopped in front of where

we were hanging on. "Come," it said. Its voice was low and clear. Its deep purple eyes looked directly into mine.

I pulled myself forward, using my arms to drag Becky and me back over the railing.

The Hottini barked something I didn't understand. Suddenly, we dropped.

"Ah!" Becky landed on her side, but quickly sat up, looking unhurt.

I landed on my face, and my nose and head hurt, but I also managed to sit up.

The six-legged Froms were bouncing, swarming haphazardly on the balcony and in the bay below us.

"Are you saving us?" asked Becky, looking up at the Hottini.

It stared back at her. It seemed to be smiling a little, but after what had just happened, I wasn't ready to trust anyone. I reached for Becky and helped her up, holding her close to me.

"My sibling asked if you're saving us. That's what I want to know too."

"Saving you, yes," said the Hottini. It tilted its head almost imperceptibly forward. "Stupid Froms trust Xaxor swarm." It turned back the way it had come and began walking, now much more lightly than before, though it was still wearing the heavy boots.

Becky and I followed. I just had to hope that if the Hottini were going to betray us, too, they knew how much money we were worth.

"I know it was stupid, honored Hottini," I said. "I didn't know what to do. Ip got stuck in the passage with the Masters."

"Ip explained the situation," said the Hottini. "It wished us to inform you that it is back on Earth and the Masters know nothing."

"He says Ip got away," I said to Becky. Then, to the Hottini, "Thank you for saving us, honored Hottini."

The Xaxor had mostly recovered from the shock of having the gravity back on. They were filling the balcony around us, but they opened a path to make room for us to go through. None of them made a move to stop us.

The Hottini nodded slightly here and there to the right and left, as if politely greeting acquaintances, but the Xaxor glared back menacingly. All three eyes of all the hundreds of Xaxor were watching us. There was now very little of their awful music.

After a while, we came to a door that led off from the balcony. Here the passage was free of Xaxor, and much narrower. I was just about to ask where we were going, when we turned a corner and I couldn't help but stop and gasp.

We were in a space dock, where a small ship was sitting, guarded by several more Hottini. But this was not what made me stop. The space dock ended with a window. Through it, I saw the planet beneath us. Its blue oceans were broken by thick clouds, and large land masses glowed.

"Do you see that, Becky? It's O-thʋl-ba. We're in space!"

"It's so pretty!"

"It is. You know what, I bet we're the first Earth people to ever see this."

15

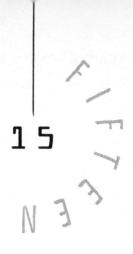

"Come," **said the Hottini** who had rescued us.

We walked forward, toward the ship and the window. I stared at the planet and the stars that lit up the sky. I wanted to take in every little detail, but there was no time. The Hottini led us up a ramp and into the belly of the ship.

Inside, there were no windows. There was barely enough room for the six Hottini in the cabin with us, so that we had to squeeze against a padded wall. The Hottini were all dressed the same as the first one, in clear coverings through which I could see their thick blue hair. All had purple eyes, although the shades ranged from light to dark. Once I was packed in with them, I became aware of a unique scent, like a mixture of spices. It wasn't exactly unpleasant, but it tickled my nose.

I felt a jolt as we lifted off the floor, and then Becky and I were thrust into the wall. The Hottini were less affected by the change and barely appeared to brace their feet. Before I'd gotten used to the movement, I fell away from the wall again.

Becky fell forward, but I caught her before she could knock into the nearest Hottini. The ramp lowered out of the cabin and clanged as it hit the floor below.

"Are we on the doggie ship?" asked Becky.

"I think so. Remember, say their name right and be polite. If you don't know what to say, let me talk."

Becky frowned, but didn't talk back.

The Hottini began filing down the ramp, heavy boots clanging. One remained with us. I thought it was the same one who had come for us, but I couldn't be sure.

"Follow," it said.

I made sure my backpack was securely on my shoulders and Becky's hand was securely in mine, and then followed the Hottini down the ramp. The aroma in the main ship was still spicy, though not quite as strong. As I stepped off the ramp, I saw to my right a window much like the one in the Xaxor ship, but smaller. Through it I could still see the planet and the stars. The Xaxor ship itself was nowhere in sight.

The Hottini space dock was much smaller than the Xaxor one. There was barely enough room for the Hottini to walk single file along the edge of the ship.

"How do you land in here?" I asked.

"We navigate better than the rest," said the Hottini. "Follow." It waited for the others to file through a low, wide door, then led us through. We were in a narrow hall, again just wide enough for one Hottini to pass.

"Where are we going?"

"The captain will deal with you." The Hottini suddenly stopped and turned its head to stare at the wall to our right. A few seconds passed. Then a piece of the wall disappeared in a flash of light, and the Hottini calmly walked into the space.

We followed it into what turned out to be a cylinder, big enough for maybe three Hottini. The wall reappeared in front of us, and the floor began to shake. We seemed to be going up. The wall disappeared again, but instead of a passage, we were now in front of a large room with its own window. Through the window, I saw that the planet was now farther away and getting smaller.

A single Hottini stood in front of the window, looking out. It was dressed differently than the others. Its covering was not see-through, but was a deep black like on TV. Everything was covered but its head. The blue hair on its head was slicked back, so that its ears appeared to stick up. They were sharp and pointy and twitched as the Hottini turned around to face us. Its eyes were the very deepest purple.

"You are Ry-an and Beck-y," said the Hottini in black, looking straight at me.

I raised my arms up and nudged Becky with my foot. She got the picture and raised her arms too. We brought them down together.

"Yes, honored Hottini captain," I said, praying I was pronouncing it right.

"I am Grav-e." He nodded at me very, very slightly.

"Gravy?" Becky whispered.

"That's right, Becky. The captain's name is Grav-e." I tried to give her my meanest look without making it obvious.

She giggled.

Grav-e growled something in their language. Suddenly the other one was behind us, wrapping a front leg around Becky's waist.

She screamed.

The Hottini pulled her away from me, holding her in midair.

"Ow! Stop!" Becky kicked her legs, and the Hottini wrapped one of his hind legs around them. He seemed to have no trouble at all standing on just two legs, one front and one hind.

I raised my arms again. "We are infinitely sorry. Becky is too young to understand." No, she wasn't. Why couldn't she just keep it together? I struggled to keep my face calm.

Grav-e turned back to the window. The planet was now a tiny speck in the distance, but I could still see its sun, though it was also growing smaller. "It took three hundred years of space flight to travel home, before the Masters built the tunnels," he said. I couldn't interpret his tone. It sounded flat, as if he'd forgotten about the insult. Yet the other one still held Becky in his grip.

She had stopped struggling and was now letting the tears roll down her face.

I kept my arms raised high. "What tunnels, honored Grav-e?"

"Large portals the Masters have cut through space using their knowledge of bok. They have built tunnels from O-thul-ba to our planet and between other places of their choosing. They do not tell us where all the tunnels are." Grav-e paused for a few seconds.

I wanted to lower my arms, but the ritual was only to be done facing the person of honor. Now that Grav-e had turned away, I couldn't finish it without insult.

"Watch," he said.

Suddenly, the sun and stars in the window were gone. There was total blackness. More seconds went by.

Becky and the other Hottini were both silent, also watching the window.

Grav-e turned back to me.

I brought my arms down swiftly and bowed forward.

"You have a calculator."

How did he know? I didn't know what to say, so I said nothing.

"You cannot hide such a powerful device from us." Grav-e turned the rest of his body away from the window so that he was facing me straight on. Behind him, the view was still completely dark. "We have saved you. Now you will give the calculator to us." He pulled one foot out of his boot, a much smaller boot than the gravity boots the others had been wearing. The naked foot had many fingers, and they curled toward me like a hand.

I heard footsteps behind me. I did not need to look to know that there were more Hottini out there, preventing my escape. As if I could go anywhere while they had me on a spaceship. Plus, they *had* saved us. I didn't have much of a choice.

I pulled my backpack around my shoulders and dug in it for the calculator. It was buried below the food and water, but appeared unharmed. I reached in and pulled it out. Grav-e did not move, so I walked forward and placed it in his foot.

Grav-e sat down abruptly on his haunches and pulled his other front leg out of his boot. It turned out to also have fingers. I counted eight on each foot. "Explain."

"I don't know a lot," I said. "All I know is how to get from one door to another. You push this." I took it from him and pushed the place on the top that was supposed to show the starting grid. Lines flashed across the screen, but it didn't show anything coherent. "I don't know what it does out here where there are no doors." I handed the calculator back to Grav-e.

Abruptly, the screen went off. I reached over and pushed the spot on the top again, but nothing happened. I picked it up out of Grav-e's feet. The screen came on by itself, lines flashing incoherently.

Grav-e turned his whole head to face me and nodded slightly. It was the same respectful-looking nod that the other Hottini had given to the Xaxor. It didn't make me feel better.

"It has an imprint," said Grav-e.

The Hottini holding Becky was giving me the same look. I now saw four others in the doorway, still, but watching me. Becky was crying a little, but she didn't look hurt.

"What do you mean?" I asked.

"A Master would not imprint for a From," said Grav-e. He turned his head toward the four standing in the doorway and barked something in their language.

They came forward slowly.

"I don't understand. The Masters didn't give it to me. I stole it. There's nothing wrong with it."

"You cannot imprint."

"I don't know what you mean. I didn't do anything to it."

"It works for you only."

"No, that's not . . . we're just not in the passage with the portals." I was too aware of the blackness behind me as I backed up, away from the approaching four Hottini. The cold of whatever the window was made of seeped into my back. I wondered if it was true. Did Front know enough about the calculator to make it work only for me?

One of the four Hottini barked something to Grav-e. Grav-e responded loudly. His expression didn't change much, but I knew it wasn't good. Then he turned his face to me.

"Create a map of all the tunnels." He thrust the calculator toward me. "Trade the map for your freedom."

Behind him, the view suddenly changed. The blackness was gone, and the stars had come out again.

I knew I didn't know how to do what he wanted, but I just raised my arms up and brought them down. I stared at the calculator, which looked blank and dead.

Grav-e stood up on all four feet again, gracefully placing each front foot into its boot. "Go," he said. He turned back to the window. Under the black covering he wore, the outline of a tail pressed up.

I turned to the four Hottini, who stared grimly back at me. The other one was still holding Becky tightly. "Come on, put Becky down." This was enough. I didn't like this at all.

"Ryan, what's going on?" A tear trickled down her face.

"They want me to map the Pipe Men tunnels. They're like the portals between our house and the zoo, the kind that always stay in one place, only they're big enough for spaceships to fly through. I guess the Hottini don't know where they all are. But I can't do it! I only know how to get between the doors inside the passage."

"Let me go!" She started kicking again.

Her captor barked something.

One of the other four barked something back.

Grav-e seemed to be ignoring us all, staring calmly out the window.

Then the first one turned, still carrying Becky, who was still kicking. He had some trouble walking on just two legs, but in a strange clumping way, he managed to get through the doorway. The wall began to close.

"Stop! Where are you taking it?" We couldn't get

separated. They couldn't take her. But I couldn't go any-where with four of them in front of me.

"You will make the map," said one. "Follow."

That Hottini and one other headed for the door, which opened again. The space beyond them was now empty. Becky was gone.

"Where am I going? I'm not doing anything with-out Becky!" I planted my feet.

"No map, no Beck-y." One of the Hottini wrapped a leg around my shoulders and pulled me into the eleva-tor. The spicy odor overwhelmed me, and I gasped for breath. The Hottini slowly removed his leg and turned his head away, lifting his nose high.

The wall closed in front of us. We were going up.

"I'm just trying to get medicine for my parent." I coughed. The space was too small for all of the Hottini, much less me. "I gave you what you asked for. Why are you doing this?"

The one who had grabbed me turned back toward me. He had very light lavender eyes, and his ears lay flat over the top of his head. "Do you like to be a captive of the Masters?"

The question put me off guard. "I didn't know I was

until this week. But you aren't in a zoo. You can go any-where."

"Without the power to use all the tunnels and make more, we have no freedom."

The elevator stopped, and the wall flashed open. The one who had spoken went out first, into another narrow passage.

I followed. "So the Masters control everything. So what? You can't take my sibling. You can't make me do something I don't know how to do!"

Another one put a foot out in front of me. I tripped, and he pushed me through an open door that, in my anger, I hadn't even noticed.

The one who had spoken poked his head into the doorway. "We will not hurt the child."

Then the wall closed in front of me. I was staring at what looked like solid metal, still holding the useless calculator in my hand.

16

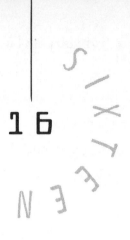

I STOOD THERE FOR what felt like minutes, staring at the door. I wanted to beat on it, but I knew it wouldn't help. I was on a ship probably billions of miles from home, surrounded by Froms who had Becky and refused to let me go unless I did something I couldn't do. I gripped the calculator so tightly that its edges dug into my skin.

Suddenly, I heard a humming sound.

I jumped and whipped around. The room was not large, but there was enough space to walk. There was no furniture. In a corner, a Xaxor sat. Its body rested on the ground, all six of its legs splayed out in front of it, its top two sections leaning sadly forward. Its legs rubbed against each other.

"Stop that! You did this! You put me here!" I wanted to punch the thing right in its three staring, grotesque eyes. But it looked so pathetic, all splayed out like that, that I just sat down on the opposite side of the room. I tried to stop the tears from coming, tried to get my mind together. I had to think of something.

The Xaxor slowly stumbled to its feet. Unsteadily, it walked toward me. It did not have the light step they'd had before, and its eyes didn't quite seem to focus. It reached me and dropped heavily, a mess of hair and legs. Weakly, it lifted one of the legs high and seemed to be pointing backward.

"Whatever it is, I don't care."

It kept pointing.

I sighed and peeked over its head to see what it was pointing at. On its back, it wore a black cloak, the same as the kind the first Xaxor I'd met had been wearing. There was a slight opening in the cloak.

"You want me to go in there?"

The Xaxor blinked at me.

I put the calculator down and reached over the Xaxor's head. I hesitated before sticking my hand into the opening, but I did it. Immediately, I felt something hard and cold. I pulled it out and sat back against the wall again. It was the tablet device that we had used to communicate before.

"Are you the same one that tricked me into going on your ship?" I put the device down in front of it.

Laboriously, it typed the answer.

Yes. I am sorry.

"You're sorry? Why, because they're doing to you what you tried to do to me?"

The Xaxor lowered its eyes and folded its legs inward.

"And now you're being nice to me again because you want my help. Well, I can't help you! I'm trapped here just like you are. I'm supposed to use this"—I pointed at the calculator—"to map all the tunnels through space the Masters made. But I don't know how to do it. I can't do it. And now they have Becky and my parent's going to die and I'm never going back to Earth. I'm probably never going to see another Earth person in my whole life!" I put my hands over my face. I just wanted to block everything out. I sat there for a while, until I felt a gentle nudging. The Xaxor was pressing the tablet against my leg.

I can help you.

"How? Have you ever seen one of these before?" I waved the calculator.

No, but we avoid the Hottini. I know of more tunnels than they do. Its eyes stared at me.

"How will they know I don't have all the tunnels, if there are at least some on there they haven't seen?" I said, almost to myself. "I still don't know how we'll get out, but if you help me, I'll do what I can."

The Xaxor lifted its eyelids and stared at me. It pulled the three legs still splayed behind it toward its body. I got the feeling it was smiling.

Just then, the wall opened up again. A Hottini stepped forward into the room, carrying a large tray on his back. With one foot, he swooped the tray off his back and set it on the ground. It contained what looked like a large hard-boiled egg, bigger than a basketball; a stack of dark, thick pieces of something like bread; a large bowl of water; and a rolled-up strip of Pipe Man fabric.

The Hottini kicked the egg off the tray with one booted foot. It rolled into the opposite wall and stopped with a thump.

The Xaxor whistled with its legs and stumbled to

standing. Its legs shook, and one or two slid out from under it as it awkwardly shuffled across the floor. Upon reaching the egg, it threw itself on top of it, so that its hairy lower belly rested on the flatter side. It closed its eyes and sat perfectly still, except for a very small humming that came from two of its legs fluttering together on top of the egg's surface.

"You drink this." The Hottini pointed at the stack of what looked like sliced bread.

I walked over to the tray and picked up a slice. It was as big as a regular-sized piece of paper and about an inch thick. It felt so hard, I worried I'd break my teeth on it. I also couldn't be sure I could eat anything that didn't come from Earth. "Have you had any other Earth people here?"

"Drink or starve," said the Hottini.

"Did you bring some to my sibling? Where are you keeping it?"

"Drink or starve."

I still had my backpack with some food and water, but what if I needed it later? I couldn't pass up a chance to eat. I bit into the bread. It was hard on the outside, but inside it was chewable, even though it was so dry I could barely swallow it. I knelt down and drank some of the water from the bowl. It tasted normal and clean.

The Hottini reached a foot out of one boot and picked up the rolled piece of Pipe Man fabric. With a swift shake, he unrolled the fabric onto the floor. Pricks of light came on all over its surface. The Hottini reached into his boot, pulled something out, and tossed it to me.

I caught it without thinking. It was a tightly rolled strip of fabric, pointed at the end like a pen.

"Mᴀp," said the Hottini. Without waiting for me to answer, he stepped backward through the door, leaving the tray of food. The wall closed in front of him.

I glanced over at the Xaxor. The egg was only about half its original size now. It had flattened and spread out under the Xaxor, whose three eyes were still closed. I took another bite of the hard bread and sat down on the floor to look at the Pipe Man fabric with the points of light. Were they supposed to be stars? There were brighter lights and dimmer lights. Some of the dimmer lights were clustered near the brighter ones. That made me think they were planets, but I had no idea where O-thul-ba was, or where we were now.

I retrieved the calculator from the floor where I'd left

it and sat in front of the star chart. The screen was still full of random lines. I ran my finger around the outer edges, pressing parts that stuck out from the others. Finally, the grid came back. But there were no numbers on it, nothing that meant anything to me.

I looked up to see the Xaxor moving toward me, the egg now completely gone. It was now walking without trouble, and its eyes were bright, peering at the calculator and the star chart.

"I don't know what I'm supposed to do with it," I said. "All I know is how to count doors. I don't even know where we are."

The Xaxor reached out a long, thin leg and wrapped it around the pen, lifting it from my hand. With the pen, it tapped a point on the left side of the chart. It was one of the lighter dots, a planet.

"Is that O-thul-ba?"

The Xaxor shook its head, then turned the pen and pointed to itself.

"It's your home?"

The Xaxor nodded awkwardly, twisting its top section as it bent it forward.

"Okay, we might as well start there. There's a tunnel from your planet to O-thul-ba?"

It nodded.

"Well, where's O-thul-ba?"

The Xaxor hesitated, then shook its head.

"Do you recognize any of the other planets?"

It typed, Near Xaxor, but none with Froms. It pointed to a spot near one of the stars closest to Xaxor. The tunnel is here.

"How do they expect me to do this if O-thul-ba isn't even on here?"

The Xaxor tapped the tunnel near Xaxor with the pen. A light appeared three eyes above the chart, floating in midair. The Xaxor then tapped the left edge of the chart. The picture changed. It now showed different stars, different planets. But there was no way I'd recognize any of them. The Xaxor tapped the edge again, examined the new pattern of stars, then tapped again. Finally it tapped another planet.

"O-thul-ba?"

It nodded.

A light for O-thul-ba appeared above the chart.

The Xaxor took the pen and drew a line in the air between them. As it did so, a blue line of light appeared, connecting the two points.

"Can you mark any of the others?"

The Xaxor nodded and tapped O-thul-ba again. One by one, it tapped other planets, some of them so far away from one another that it had to change the screen of the star chart ten, twenty, or thirty times before reaching the second point. After a while, the air was filled with blue lines and glowing lights. But all the points ended at O-thul-ba.

"Aren't there any others?"

These are all we know.

"Do you know where Earth is?"

It shook its head.

The wall opened up again, and two Hottini stepped through into the room. One came over to us and examined the map floating in the air. He glanced disdainfully at the calculator.

"Only Xaxor knowledge," he said. He turned his eyes to the Xaxor. "Does not change anything." The Hottini turned to me. "Map the rest." He turned around and, with his companion, disappeared back into the wall.

"What did it mean by 'does not change anything'?" I asked.

It means they won't release me. They are taking me to their home world to be punished.

"For what? Why do they care what you did to me?"

I'm sure they don't care about you. They care about their pride. We insulted them by kidnapping you.

"Are they going to put you in jail?"

No one knows what the Hottini do. The Xaxor sat down heavily, folding all its legs beneath it, and closed two of its eyes. The third one watched the map we'd made, still floating in the air.

"I'll figure out some way to make this work," I said. I didn't know how finishing the map would help the Xaxor, but it was still my only chance of getting Becky and me to the Brocine. I ran my hand along the edges of the calculator again, pressing in every little bump.

17

THE SCREEN WAS LIT UP, but it was just a blank grid without any numbers. There didn't seem to be any way to connect the grid to the points of light on the star chart.

The Xaxor peered at it.

It seemed like hours since any of the Hottini had been back to see us. They could come back at any minute.

The Xaxor touched the calculator with two legs, looking up at me.

"Go ahead, but it's not going to work." I let the Xaxor lift the calculator out of my hands and sat down on the floor. I took another bite of bread. It was still dry and tasteless.

The Xaxor lifted the calculator with two delicate legs

and pushed it slowly through the map hanging in the air before us. It poked my shoulder with a third leg.

Sighing, I got to my feet again and reached out to take it. The light from the map made my hand blue. As soon as I touched the calculator, it started vibrating.

The Xaxor turned one eye toward me. It was bouncing on the three legs that held it up.

I had to lean forward to see exactly what was going on. The calculator's screen was now filled with dots. Could these represent stars? If they did, I still didn't know which one was which. Angrily, I poked at the screen. Something had to be better than nothing.

Suddenly, the star chart was gone—and so was my right hand and the calculator. At least, I couldn't see them. They were in the middle of the blackness, the door through space that had just opened in front of us.

The Xaxor bounced and waved its legs at me, pointing toward the door.

"That's great, but it's not a map of all the tunnels."

The Xaxor typed quickly. I have to go. This is my only chance.

"You don't even know where it goes to. I just poked a random spot. You might not even be able to breathe."

They will probably kill me. And you.

"I can't leave without Becky."

The Xaxor looked at me with all three eyes. *I am sorry I tried to sell you. I wish you well.*

"Thanks. You too."

The Xaxor stuffed the tablet into its cloak and gave me a last look. Then it stepped into the blackness.

Just as its last leg disappeared, the wall opened up again. Two Hottini rushed toward me. I poked the screen, hoping to shut the portal down, but nothing happened.

One Hottini pulled his foot out of his boot and reached out for me.

Without thinking, I tried to jump out of the way, tripped, and fell forward. I dropped the calculator and caught myself with my hands. They sank into the ground. I was not on the Hottini ship. I rolled over onto my backpack. The portal was still there.

I looked around for the calculator and saw it a foot away, half sunk into the soft reddish-brown dirt. I grabbed it and was about to run back through when I felt something touch me. It was the Xaxor's leg. It blinked at me.

"I have to go back," I said.

It shook its head vigorously.

"I told you, I can't leave my sibling."

It shook its head again and pulled out the tablet.

Anxiously, I eyed the door. What if it disappeared?

The ship is moving. What if the door is no longer on it?

"I came through after you. We came to the same place, didn't we?" But what if the Xaxor was right? I didn't know anything about how this worked. What if I stepped back through into empty space? I stood there staring at the Xaxor, not sure what to do. "I can't just do nothing!"

You can open a door to one of the Brocine planets. If that machine can open doors, you don't need the Hottini.

"But I don't know how to do it! I just punched a random spot."

We have time to work on it.

"Do we? They have my sibling! Is there nutrition here? Is there water? Are there any round white things for you to drink? We don't even know where we are!" I shouted the last line in English, not caring if it understood me.

"Don't you recognize my home?"

I spun around, searching for the voice.

The Xaxor turned its head, flitting its eyes this way and that.

"I am not here. You are on the opposite side of Frontringhor."

"Front?"

"Has the Earth been here?" said a different voice.

I stared at the Xaxor. "Did you speak?"

It stared back. *"I thought."*

"You think in English?"

"What is English?"

"I am translating," said Front's voice in my head. It didn't sound quite like the physical voice that I remembered. It was more clear, less deep.

I was looking away from the door now, out into the landscape. There were clouds, but it was much lighter than it had been near Front's cave. The landscape was even more uniform, a seemingly endless expanse of the same soft dirt we were standing in. A few tall, thin trees with a few twisted branches stood here and there.

"Front! How did we get here? How can I get back on the ship?"

"You have found my escape hatch. I set it to return here in case you were in danger."

"Is it safe to go back through?"

"It is safe, but—"

The Xaxor let out a shrieking hum.

I spun around and saw half of a Hottini. His head and front legs were on Frontringhor, but the rest of him was still in blackness.

"Go back!" I cried.

Instead, he jumped through and tackled me. The Xaxor sprang onto the Hottini's back, and the Hottini growled, pulled one foot out of his boot, and grabbed the Xaxor. With one strong tug, he wrenched the Xaxor off his back and hurled it, sending it flying like a football, screeching.

The Hottini wrapped me up with his front legs and lifted me right off the ground, standing straight up on two feet, then pulled me backward into the blackness.

I kicked it.

Then, with a growl, it dropped me. I landed with my face in the soft dirt.

"It is a one-way door," said Front's voice.

"Who said that?"

I rolled over, coughing the dirt out of my mouth, to find the Hottini glaring regally down at me.

In the distance, the Xaxor was limping back toward us, holding one leg close to its body.

The Hottini glared at me. "Open the door back."

"I don't know how."

He closed the two feet between us and stuck his nose up against mine. The spicy smell was distinctly pungent, and the anger in his purple eyes made me turn my face away.

"I really don't know. I want to get back, too! You have my sibling."

"You got here somehow."

"It was an accident."

"You!" the Hottini shouted. "Xaxor! Undo this!"

"Eat my eyelids," said the Xaxor.

The Hottini shot a look at me. "How is it talking?"

I shrugged, not sure what Front wanted me to say.

"Since we are all here," said Front, *"I would like us all to understand each other."*

The Hottini took a step backward and looked around.

"Tast-e, member of the Hottini guard, meet Ryan, a boy from the O-thul-ban zoo, and one of the Xaxor, a species that does not give names."

"I know all about the Xaxor." Tast-e glared at it, and the Xaxor glared back.

"Front, I have to go back for Becky! Please help us get back to the Hottini ship!"

Tast-e looked around him, still trying to find the source of the strange voice. "Are you responsible for this? Where are you?"

I held the calculator in front of me. "Tell me what to do to get back to the ship!" I was almost ready to cry. The ship was getting farther and farther away from where we'd left it.

"It is all right, Ryan. The calculator will take you where you need to go. It remembers every place where it's been activated."

"It's not all right. They could be hurting her now that I'm gone. I have to get back!"

"No one is going to hurt the child," said Tast-e.

"That's so reassuring, coming from you," I snapped.

The Xaxor limped closer to Tast-e, glaring up at him.

"Look, whoever you are. We're all in agreement that we must go back to the ship," said Tast-e.

The Xaxor glared and shook its head vigorously.

"Well, everyone who matters agrees."

"You will have to wait a short time. I would like to see Ryan again. Please hold the calculator up, Ryan."

I lifted it up so I was staring at its face. The screen was glowing, but it was blank.

"Press the upper right-hand corner."

I did, and a series of date and time notations appeared, in Pipe Man script.

"The time stamps mark the places where the calculator has been activated. The Hottini ship will be the most recent."

"Oh, thank you!"

"The calculator was last activated on my side of Frontringhor at 18:16, day 186."

I scrolled down a few screens and found the time and day Front was talking about. Finally, something that made sense. I glanced at the Xaxor. "Front wants me to go see him. Will you be all right here?"

The Xaxor glared up at Tast-e. *"This thing will behave, or it is not getting a ride back to its ship."*

I looked pointedly at Tast-e. "That's right. If you hurt the Xaxor again, I'll leave without you. Whatever it is you doggies drink, I doubt it grows here."

Tast-e said nothing, but sat down carefully on his

haunches, staring calmly ahead. Probably, he didn't know what doggies were.

"Good. Okay, Front, here I come." I pressed the time stamp. Sure enough, a door of complete blackness appeared in the air in front of me. I nodded at the Xaxor and stepped through.

18

I WAS OUT IN THE SWAMP AGAIN, between the two caves we'd been in before, but it was dark here, so I could only see by starlight. Both of Front's heads stood a foot in front of me. All five antennae leaned forward, close enough to touch me. Both mouths were even across the faces, not smiling or frowning. The necks stretched out behind each head, followed by bodies going so far back that, in the dark, I couldn't see where they connected.

Then both mouths turned up in smiles. "It's good to see you again, Ryan," the head on the left said. The head on the right just smiled at me, not moving. "But tell me, how did it come that you needed to escape?"

I told him about how the Xaxor had kidnapped us and the Hottini had rescued us, only to lock us up and insist that I use the calculator to help them. I hesitated, trying to figure out how to tell him that I'd actually tried to give away the calculator. I forgot that Front was telepathic.

"It is all right, Ryan," said Front. "You thought you had to do it."

"I didn't know it could actually open a portal," I said. I hung my head, not able to look at him. I wanted to ask him why he didn't tell me, but I knew. I'd been in such a hurry to leave the first time. "Did you really set it up so I'm the only one who can use it?"

"It seemed safer that way. In case it falls into the wrong hands."

"Wouldn't it be better if everyone could open portals instead of just the Pipe Men?" I asked.

"If everyone could come to Earth and kidnap its people? If everyone could strip primitive planets of resources?" Front spoke with his left-side head, which smiled, but the right-side head frowned, its three antennae drooping.

I hadn't thought about that. "But how did you even

know how to make it only work for me? The Pipe Men wouldn't teach you that."

The smile on the left-side head grew bigger. "I understand þok better than the Pipe Men. Someday when we have more time, I will explain it all." The right-side head smiled a little. Then the left-side head spoke again. "I would have taught you how to make a portal, but I did not want to put you in danger. It was not time."

"I'm in danger now! Please, teach me how we can get to the Brocine planets. And then home!"

"I will teach you. But you cannot give the calculator away."

"Why does it matter, if no one else can use it?"

"They can take it apart," said the right-side head, its mouth straight and grim. Two of its three antennae reached out toward me. "They must not learn what is inside it."

"All right," I said. "I won't give it to them." I would really have to find a way to escape the Hottini now. "Please, tell me how to get to one of the Brocine planets, and how to do it fast, because I'm going to have to grab Becky and run."

Front reached out one antenna from its left-side head and tapped me lightly on the chest. "I will not let anything happen to you or Becky if I can help it. Here is what you need to do. Your calculator has never been to the Brocine native system. This means you will have to calculate the point in space."

I stared down at the calculator. It was showing a blank grid.

"The calculator draws on the essence of þok. At its core, þok is life. The Brocine systems are a concentrated burst of life. They live far from here, but once you are onboard the Hottini ship, you will be much closer. You will find the Brocine where there is the largest concentration of froms within billions of miles. Run your finger under the calculator, top left corner to bottom right."

I did it, and the screen lit up with dots. Some were bright, but others were so dim that they were barely there.

"Brush from left to right over the middle of the screen to change the picture." Front cocked both heads, and both smiled.

"The biggest dot?"

The left-side head nodded. "There will be many large dots, concentrated in a cluster. The very largest dot will be Brock itself, the main Brocine planet. This is all I have time to teach you now. But one thing is very important. When you are ready to leave Brock, you must not go by spaceship. No matter what happens, you must use the calculator to open a portal."

"Why?"

"I will explain everything someday. Please trust me," said Front, "and promise."

It seemed like the best idea anyway. "I promise. Thank you, Front!" I reached down and threw my arms around both heads together.

One of Front's antennae tapped my head. "Good luck, Ryan. Come back whenever you need to."

"I will, thank you." I looked behind me. The door from the other side of the planet was still there, but around it, I could just see the entrance to one of the caves in the starlight. I knew there was a portal in there, one that would take me close to home. But I couldn't go back yet. What if I couldn't go back at all?

"The future will not be what you expect," said Front, reading my mind.

"I know." I tried to shake it off.

"Go safely," said Front, beginning the traditional Pipe Man goodbye.

"And hold your eyes still," I finished. I took one last look at Front, whose heads were now both smiling at me, then stepped into the portal.

19

THE XAXOR WAS STANDING IN FRONT of Tast-e, almost close enough to touch the Hottini with its eye-balls. It was still holding one of its legs against its body. As I stepped through the portal, the Xaxor turned one eye to look at me.

Tast-e took a few long seconds to continue glaring at the Xaxor, then turned his head slowly. "Well, have you learned how to get off this wretched planet?"

The Xaxor rubbed its legs furiously, causing a screeching hum. It turned a second eye to me.

"So you agree on something now?"

Both Froms glared at me, without taking their eyes off each other.

"I can't stay here, but I'm not going back to that ship either," said the Xaxor.

"You can come with me," I said, "but we have to go back to the ship first. Once we get out of there safely, we'll figure out how to send you home."

The Xaxor turned its middle eye back toward the Hottini, then blinked at me with the single eye still facing me.

"And you're not going to stop us," I said to Tast-e.

He slowly turned his full glare toward me.

"I don't have to take you back with me," I said.

"I doubt you have learned how to close the portal behind you."

"Press the same button again," said Front's voice in my head.

"I know more than you think I know," I said, standing up as tall as possible. "If you try to stop us, I'll send you back here, or someplace worse. I once went to a planet with no air."

Tast-e slowly raised himself to all four feet, much more gracefully than expected from something that looked like a blue dog. He left the Xaxor and walked right up to me, almost pressing his nose against mine. "My fellows would hunt you down."

I shoved the calculator in between my face and his and pressed the right-hand corner, too hard. The time stamps appeared on the screen. I pressed the one for the Hottini ship.

The Hottini's purple eyes widened, and then his whole body was replaced by blackness.

"Maybe it's lost in space," said the Xaxor, limping over to me.

"Yeah, maybe." I doubted it. That would be too good to be true.

The Xaxor pointed all its eyes at me. *"Before I lose the ability to speak to you, shall we talk about a plan?"*

"I'm going to act like I really know how to use this thing and I could send any one of them to some far-off planet, like what I did to Tast-e just now. You just stick by me and act like you believe it."

"Well thought out."

"And your plan to sell me to the highest bidder worked out great. You have something better?"

The Xaxor hung its head over its middle section.

"I didn't think so."

It looked up at me. *"It was nice talking to you."*

"Yeah." I turned and looked around at the barren landscape. "Thank you, Front. I'll be back to see you when I can."

"Hold your eyes still, Ryan."

"You too."

The Xaxor was looking down again.

"Hey, it's okay. I forgave you already for all that. Just stick by me and act like I know what I'm doing, okay?"

"Okay." It held out a leg toward the portal, waving me forward. I stepped through.

The room was full of Hottini. Tast-e was standing in front, his mouth curled into a smile. The Xaxor's top section and three legs appeared through the blackness of the portal. It hesitated for a second, then stepped all the way through.

I pressed the same spot again. With a slight whoosh of air, the portal closed behind us. I held the calculator up and gave Tast-e my best sure-of-myself look.

"Take me to Becky! Or I'll open another one right in your face. And you don't want to know where you'll be going."

Nobody moved.

"Then bring Becky here!" I yelled, waving the calculator at them.

A door in the wall flashed open, and I heard a giggle. I couldn't believe what I saw. There was Becky, looking happy as ever, sitting right on top of Grav-e's back, clutching his black cloak like a rein.

The other Hottini looked just as surprised as I was. Even Tast-e lost all interest in me as he stared at Grav-e, who stared back at all of us with a slight smile.

"It asked to ride," he said.

There was complete silence as Grav-e bent at his knees, allowing Becky to clamber off.

She ran toward me. "Ryan!"

I grabbed her and hugged her, then pushed her away, looking at her up and down. She seemed okay, if a little dirty, and she was smiling.

"They made me eat stale crackers, but then we played hopscotch."

"These guys played hopscotch?"

"They hop on one leg better than I do!"

"Okay, that's nice, Becky, but you have to listen to me. We're not going to stay with them. We're going to go now. You have to just trust me and follow me, okay?"

"Can we take one of the doggies with us?" She turned and flashed a smile at Grav-e.

Grav-e had recovered his regal air and was now glaring lasers at us with his deepest purple eyes. The other

Hottini had formed a half circle around us and were moving slowly forward.

The Xaxor tapped lightly on my back with one leg.

I ran my finger underneath the calculator like Front had showed me. The dots appeared. Quickly, I found the biggest one and pressed it.

Grav-e barked in their language, just as a portal appeared between them and us.

Before I could say anything, Becky jumped through it. I jumped after her. She screamed. I hit my head on something and fell to my knees. I tried to stand and hit my head again. Everything was dark. I reached out and felt Becky's leg.

"It's okay, don't worry, we'll figure out where we are."

The Xaxor's body pressed against my back. Its legs were flailing. I had barely moved at all and realized it could still be half inside the portal.

"Becky, can you crawl forward? Don't worry, we're on a Brocine planet. They're going to help us." I hoped it was true. They certainly weren't expecting us to show up this way.

"Okay." She was sniffling a little, but she moved forward.

I followed, still keeping a grip on her leg.

The Xaxor wrapped a leg around my neck. I had to get the portal closed. I punched at the calculator, and it lit up, showing the same screen as before. I twisted my head around, wrapped in the Xaxor's leg, and saw that its third section was missing and its middle section was stretching painfully into the blackness.

"Hang on, I'm closing it!" I pressed the largest dot again.

The Xaxor flew into me, covering me with its legs and stench and knocking me into Becky. She screamed and crawled forward, and I was still being pushed, squooshing into her faster than she could move. Someone barked loudly.

"Becky, move!" I held on to her leg, pushing her forward, scrambling away from the noise. The calculator screen went black, leaving us in complete darkness again.

"You will pay! So many times, Earth! You will be sorry!"

"I didn't mean to take you with us. You didn't have to try and stop us! Are you Grav-e?"

"I am Tast-e!"

"Tasty?" Becky giggled in the darkness.

"That's right, Becky, its name is Tasty, like something you drink!"

Tast-e growled.

The Xaxor was trying to remove its legs from me. It hopped and flailed as I dragged it.

"Where have you taken us?" Tast-e growled.

"It's Brock," I said. "I just don't know where we are."

"Idiot From! Stop moving."

"Becky, stop." I stopped moving and tried to sit. Something about Tast-e's voice made me trust him on that point.

"We are in their private tunnels. We will not want them to find us here."

20

WE SAT IN SILENCE for a minute. Even Becky said nothing. I could hear her panting a little. I let go of her leg and felt around, finally finding her hand. I took in the dampness of the tunnel we were in, the heaviness of the humid air. It was hot, and I was starting to sweat.

"Since you apparently know nothing, I will explain our situation to you," said Tast-e. "The Brocine are smaller than all three of our species, which explains why we are cramped into little balls and forced to crawl like vermin. Visitors are normally shuttled to special spaces for big froms. They don't allow others in these tunnels. No loss to us." Tast-e sniffed disdainfully. "You already know that the Brocine have a natural weapon on their noses. What do you think will happen when we surprise them in their private tunnels?"

The Xaxor rustled. Suddenly, a dim white light appeared between us. With one leg the Xaxor was holding a small instrument, which gave off just enough light for me to see beyond it into the Hottini's haughty purple eyes.

"Well, what was I supposed to do?" I whisper-shouted. "You were holding us captive!"

"Open the portal again, and get us out of here!" Tast-e leaned over the Xaxor and pressed his face so close to mine that I could smell the strange spices of his breath again.

The Xaxor pushed itself up, forcing Tast-e's face back. It smelled worse than the Hottini, but I appreciated the support.

Becky stuck her face next to mine, confronting the Xaxor. "Say you're sorry!"

"It is sorry," I said. "The Hottini had it locked up, so it's learned its lesson. It's been helping me."

"I thought you were nice! But you wanted to sell us!"

The Xaxor pulled backward, pressing closer to Tast-e.

"It really is sorry. Anyway, we're stuck with both of them, so let's not kill each other, okay?"

"Their language sounds like screeching," Tast-e said. "At least you Xaxor keep your mouths shut."

The Xaxor rapped Tast-e on the head with its light.

Tast-e growled like a wolf.

Becky giggled.

I sighed. "Look, we need to be on this planet, and this tunnel is where the calculator sent us. When we find someone, we'll just explain what happened. They can't be any worse than the Hottini or the Xaxor." I glared at each of them in turn.

"Your lives were never in danger with us," said Tast-e.

"Right." I turned to Becky. "You remember how Dad got poked, and that's how he got sick? You have to be very careful. If you see a Brocine, you don't go toward it. You say, 'I am infinitely sorry,' just like you would to a Pipe Man, okay?"

Tast-e snorted.

"Maybe I will open the portal back to that planet with no air." I held up the calculator. "I remember just where it was."

Suddenly the tunnel was filled with noises. Scraping, scratching, breathing.

"We are infinitely sorry!" Becky and I cried at the same time.

The Brocine were all around us. I couldn't see much in the dim light, but they stank like rust, sharp and pungent and metallic. I could feel the heat from their bodies and hear the chatter of their voices as they talked to each other in their squeaky language. They sounded excited, but at least they didn't poke us with their noses.

"Does anyone speak the Masters' language?" asked Tast-e. His voice was surprisingly calm after the warning he'd just given us.

They pushed in closer, squeezing between me and the Xaxor and climbing between Becky and me. They did look like rats. Large, hairy rats wearing tiny, stinky clothes. One of them crawled on top of the Xaxor's head and grabbed the light out of its hand. Abruptly, we were in darkness again.

"You don't belong here!" said a squeaky voice.

"Oh, bless my eyes, you do speak it." I sighed with relief. At least we could explain ourselves. "We didn't mean to be here. I'm Ryan and this is my sibling, Becky.

We're from the zoo on O-thul-ba," I explained. "You have people held there, too."

"Did you think you could open a portal in our territory without us noticing?" said the same voice.

"No, I—"

"Stop. Follow us."

There was more shuffling and scratching. The Brocine skittered away from us, in the direction we had been heading.

"They stink," Becky whispered.

"Shhh." I grabbed on to her hand and began crawling. The Brocine were still around us. Though I couldn't see, it felt like they were on the walls and ceiling of the tunnel. It was the heat and the rusty metal smell.

The Xaxor hummed a little as it shuffled behind us, but Tast-e was completely silent. I took that as a good sign. If he kept his mouth shut, he couldn't say anything that would make them angry. None of the Brocine spoke either, and we crawled on in silence for what seemed like hours, though it might have been only minutes.

"You all right?" I whispered to Becky.

"Yes."

The way she said it, all quiet, made me realize she

wasn't. I wasn't feeling too good myself. The dirt from the tunnel floor that had seemed soft at first was now digging into my hands, and the knees of my leggings were worn through, so that I could feel the rough wetness on my knees.

A drop of water fell on my head, then another. Then another.

The chattering of our Brocine guides picked up.

The drops began falling thicker and harder, and soon the water was rising over my hands.

"Is the tunnel going to flood?" I finally asked.

More chatter I didn't understand.

I heard a thump behind me.

"Eep!" Becky squealed.

"What happened?"

"Get it off me!"

I reached out a hand and felt the hairy belly of the Xaxor where Becky should be.

"Ick!"

"It just slipped. Xaxor? Just move slowly, okay? Can you slide back off?"

Becky crashed into me, and the Xaxor let out a frantic hum.

"Get off me! Haven't you ever experienced a little water?" Tast-e shouted.

The humming increased, so that I had to cover my ears. Then the Brocine were crawling over me, chattering like crazy.

"Ryan, they're *on* me!"

A Brocine hit me in the face.

"Becky, don't throw them!"

"Ahhhh!"

The path fell out from under me. Water was everywhere. I had to close my mouth and hold my breath. I flailed around, trying to find Becky, but found nothing but water and dirt and rocks and Brocine. They were crawling around me, holding on somehow to the sides of the path, while I was sliding out of control. Their chattering stayed the same, like normal conversation.

I wanted to yell at them, ask what was going on, but there was water everywhere, and I couldn't open my mouth. My hand knocked against something that didn't feel like Brocine, and I couldn't tell if it was Becky or Tast-e or the Xaxor, and I was falling faster and faster, so I gave up and just let myself slide. Once I stopped flailing around, I slid faster.

It felt like many more minutes of falling, all the time trying to keep my mouth closed and spitting water out and hoping Becky was calm enough to keep her mouth closed, too. After a long while, the tunnel began to flatten and my sliding began to slow, but the water kept falling all around me. It was coming from behind me in the tunnel, and from above me, and even seemed to be seeping out of the path itself.

"Becky, are you all right?" I sputtered.

"Its legs are all over me again!"

"Kindly remove your appendages from my face, Xaxor," said Tast-e.

"I guess they don't like water. Hang on, Xaxor, I'm going to get you off them."

A spindly leg hit me in the face.

"Hold still!" I lifted the leg from my face as gently as I could and tried to follow it back to the Xaxor, but the leg slipped out of my hand, and I heard a stale, soggy humming. I sighed. "What is going on? Where are you taking us?"

All at once, the sky lit up. A pattern like stars peppered the ceiling. It was not much light, but it was enough for me to see the cavern full of Brocine. I would never be able to count how many. They were everywhere. All along the sides of a cave as big as a basketball court, they were piled on top of each other. They piled against the walls and also flowed into the floor of the cavern, many Brocine deep. Brocine ran from all sides of the cave, over the tops of each other, toward the center, where a pile of them rose high above the others in the center of the cavern floor. Water dripped from the ceiling, seeming to come from the "stars" above us, and the whole thing stank. I couldn't make out individual features, but I saw noses. Noses everywhere.

"You opened a portal." The voice was deep and loud. It seemed to be coming from the center of the room and the large pile, though I couldn't see any individual talking.

I sloshed forward. The water was up past my ankles, and I could only go a few feet, because there were too many Brocine, too many noses that I didn't want to come in contact with. "I had to! The Hottini locked me and my sibling up. I didn't know my machine would send us here. I thought it would send us to a . . . a spaceport or something."

The Xaxor gave a soggy hum.

"I have to help my friend." I slogged back to the others. Becky was gingerly picking a leg off of herself, while the Xaxor sank listlessly into the water. Tast-e stood silent, staring ahead at the pile of Brocine. I turned back to them. "My friend the Xaxor, it doesn't like the water. Please, can't you help me get it out?"

"How did you make the portal?"

"I have a calculator. I can open portals for you, too, if you want." I pulled the calculator out of my bag. It was soaking wet, and I had no idea if it would still work. "Please, help the Xaxor."

Brocine came out of the water from beneath me, splashing me and the calculator more. They pushed the Xaxor up and held it above the water, but it tipped, legs sagging into the water, so that more Brocine had to lift it. They moved away into the cave, carrying the Xaxor farther than the light of the "stars" went.

"Where are you taking it?"

"Aboveground," said the deep voice. "You are Ry-an, the child sent from O-thul-ba. And you are Tast-e, the Hottini soldier."

Tast-e stayed still and quiet. I was about to answer for both of us, when the voice continued.

"The Hottini have been in contact. They demand the release of their soldier and the transfer of their prisoners back to their ship."

"We weren't supposed to be their prisoners. They were supposed to help us."

"We have no intention of giving you back, as long as you give us the calculator."

Of course they'd want it, too. Of course! I tried not to show how frustrated I was. "I can give it to you, but it won't work. Someone imprinted it to work only for me. That's why the Hottini locked us up. They wanted me to make a map of all the Masters' tunnels, but I don't know how." I couldn't give it to them. I'd promised Front *twice*.

The pack of Brocine pulled more closely together. As one, they leaned closer. I heard sloshing. The water rippled around my feet. I stepped backward, made sure I was in front of Becky.

"Then you will stay with us, and you will learn how to use it."

No, no, no! "What about your people in the zoo? I can help you rescue them if you give me the antidote for your poison. One of your people poked my parent!"

The pack leaned forward even more. Its voice came from all around me. "We will save your parent. We will bring back our people. And you will stay here."

"No, I can't stay here, I—"

"Aah!" Becky screeched.

I tried to keep my grip on her hand, but the water made everything slippery, and she fell away. I turned around and saw her on her back, being lifted by a pack of Brocine. "Hey, stop it!" My legs went out from under me, and I fell backward. The landing was surprisingly soft, like falling on a lumpy mattress. I spit water out of my mouth and had to close my eyes because of the splashing.

When I opened my eyes again, it was almost totally dark. We were moving through another tunnel.

"Becky, are you all right?"

"I'm okay." Her voice was close.

"Hey, we can walk, you know, you don't have to carry us."

"This will be faster," said a small voice.

"Tast-e, are you here?"

"Without dignity," said Tast-e. His voice came from behind me.

"It can't be that much farther. Right?"

There was no answer, but we slowly came to a stop. There was a screeching noise and then a light so bright, I had to close my eyes again. The Brocine underneath me were not moving, but I felt myself being lifted and lifted, and the air around me changed from musty to fresh, like I was aboveground. The Brocine tickled me a little as they rolled out from under me, leaving me lying on my back on something hard.

I opened my eyes.

21

SQUEAKS, GROWLS, CHEERING, CLAPPING, and gurgling laughter filled my ears. I sat up and blinked, trying to adjust to the light.

"Food!" Becky was already standing, hopping a little with excitement.

We were at one end of a large hall. The ceiling must have been a hundred eyes up, and it was made of glass, showing a red sky dotted with white clouds. In front of us were long tables with benches on either side, set at the right height for Earth people. The benches were filled with Brocine, and they were the ones cheering.

They were wearing all different kinds of clothes, looking clean and dry. They clapped their paws together. And Becky was right—there was food. Bowls and bowls lined the tables, with things poking out of them. I couldn't tell what any of it was exactly.

"I have been here before," said Tast-e. "This is their show for other Froms."

At the far end of the hall, past the tables, a pack of maybe fifty Brocine were stacked like a pyramid. It spoke in the same deep voice I'd heard before. "Welcome to Brock, Earth people. Please, drink."

In front of the pyramid pack, a group of Brocine slid off the benches with a tiny thump, leaving an opening just big enough for Becky and me. I took a glance at Tast-e, who was standing as regally as possible, considering his drenched appearance. He didn't move or acknowledge me.

"Come on," I said, reaching for Becky's hand. I led her forward, between the benches.

All around us, the Brocine continued making noises. They began jumping from the benches onto the tables. Their noses pointed at us, but their eyes were bright and seemed friendly.

We came to the space they'd left for us and climbed onto the bench. Becky grabbed a bowl and pulled out the first thing. It resembled a cucumber, but it was striped with purple and a little fuzzy. She brought it toward her mouth.

"Wait!" I stopped her hand and looked around me. The Brocine were all on top of the table now, digging into the various items in the bowls, gripping with their claws and tearing the food with greenish, razor-sharp teeth. They seemed to be eating everything. "Let me try it first." I took it from her and sank my teeth in. It was bittersweet, like both vegetable and fruit.

"That's mine!" She grabbed it back from me and took a bite herself. "Weird!" She kept eating, slurping at the juices that dripped onto the table.

I picked up something out of the bowl in front of me. It was round and flat and reddish brown. I took a hesitant bite and found that it was crunchy, a little salty, and also a little sweet.

I felt a tapping on my leg. The Brocine next to me was eating as if nothing had happened, so I twisted around on the bench. Standing behind me, on the floor, a Brocine was looking up with big round yellow eyes. He was dressed in a black one-piece suit with buttons down the front, and his thin ears stuck back from his head, giving him a distressed look.

"Ryan Earth," he said. His voice was somewhat high, but not quite squeaky. His eyes flitted to Becky, then back to me. "My name is Gript. I am . . . that is . . ." Gript's eyes filled with water.

The Brocine next to me stopped eating and jumped down onto the bench. "It is Gript's children who were taken by the Masters." His eyes, too, filled with water.

"I'm sorry," I said.

"Have you seen them? Are they all right?" Gript's tears were flowing freely now, dripping onto his buttons.

"I've never seen them myself," I said, "but my parent—"

"It was an accident!" Gript cried. "It must have been. They would never hurt anyone!"

The one on the bench reached down a clawed paw to Gript, who clambered up next to us.

"They think it was," I said. "Your children are fine. I'm sure they are." I realized that I didn't know. I'd been so worried about my dad, I'd never stopped to wonder what had happened to the Brocine.

"You're my only hope. Please." Gript put a paw on my leg and gripped it with the surprisingly soft fingers under the claws. "You have to help my people rescue them."

"I will, of course."

"It poked our dad with its nose," said Becky. She leaned over me and stuck her face right in Gript's. "If you're going to carry those things around with you everywhere, you should carry the cure, too!"

"Becky, he doesn't speak English. Anyway, they were kidnapped. How were they supposed to plan for that?"

"They were on O-thul-ba when they were kidnapped. They should have had the cure with them!"

I sighed. I turned to Gript, purposely not translating everything. "You were on O-thul-ba when they were kidnapped, right?"

Gript nodded and wiped tears from his face with the backs of his paws. "I trade with the Masters. My pack grows a spice very rare in the universe. The only known source is in this system, a cold planet farthest from our sun. Far beneath the surface, there is a cave, made warm by the presence of rare radioactive minerals. The spice grows there. And the Masters like it in their soup.

"I wanted to take my children with me for the first time. My grown children, Hipptu and Scrappta, they were to take over the transport business. For my younger children, it was a chance to see the universe. We left the spaceport to see the city. I looked away for only a second, to watch an assistant pouring soup. When I turned back around, my children were far in the distance, being dragged away in a rolling cage. Six square holes like eyes for windows. Hipptu's eyes were staring through the lowest one." Gript pursed his pale lips and wrung his paws, shaking.

"The Pipe Men kidnapped them right off the street," I said to Becky. "What did you do?"

"You must understand, we do not do well alone." Gript sat down slowly onto the bench and gave a loud sniff. "We evolved in packs. We even speak as one. When we are together, we are strong. It took many years for me to handle the constant travel to O-thul-ba, with only a few fellows to combine with." He sniffed again. "My children are not trained for this."

As Gript had been speaking, the other Brocine had begun crowding around. Now they climbed on top of one another, surrounding him. Brocine on either side of him held his soggy-from-tears paws. Something changed about them. They were standing close together, all holding paws now. A sea of yellow eyes looked at me sadly, watering as though with one thought.

"This is how we should be," said a deep voice. It was coming from the pack somehow, but I didn't see a mouth move, and I couldn't pinpoint the source of the sound. It was coming from all of them at once. "Our children are lost. They will die if they do not come home."

"That's why we came here," I said. "We can save our parent and your family too."

"Not with our calculator," said Tast-e. He was standing, straight and soggy, to my right, glaring pointedly at me. He turned his gaze to the pack. "This From has agreed to give the calculator to us. If you wish to undertake this mission, you can do it by spaceship."

"No!" I said. That had been the plan at the beginning, when I hadn't known that the calculator could open portals. But Front had told me that I had to leave Brock by portal. I still didn't know why, but I'd already betrayed Front's trust enough. "I don't owe you anything."

Tast-e stuck his nose in my face. "Should we have left you with the Xaxor?"

I didn't know what to say to that. Without the Hottini, Becky and I would have been sold to the highest bidder. But what was to say that the Hottini wouldn't have done that, too? They hadn't proved to be trustworthy.

"This From must return to us," said a deep voice.

"The calculator is ours." It came from the pack that had welcomed us to the feast.

"I didn't agree to stay here," I said. I glanced at Tast-e. His imperious glare helped me make my decision. I turned to the new pack. "But I said I'd give you the calculator, and I will." I'd just have to think of some way out of it later. I hated to lie to these people, but I had to get the antidote. Mom couldn't say I was doing the wrong thing. No one could.

"If only you can use it, you must return," the pack said.

I looked at Gript's pack to see if Gript and his friends would protest, but they were silent. The chain of Brocine paws now stretched from Gript's group to the other, so that they now appeared to be speaking with only one voice.

I thought quickly. "Not until I know my parent is safe, and if you help my family escape to anywhere we want to go." I glared at Tast-e. "That's what the Hottini were supposed to do. Then if I haven't figured out how to make it work for you, I'll come back." Was there something else? Something I was forgetting? "And the Xaxor! You have to take it home, and don't let the Hottini have it."

Tast-e was glaring purple lasers at me.

"Drink, then! We will go tomorrow!" The combined pack dissolved into a melee of Brocine, who scampered toward the tables and eagerly resumed their meals.

I turned back to the group of Brocine in front of me. Now there were only Gript and a few others, still holding paws.

"We will both find our families," said Gript, in his own, small voice. Being in the pack seemed to have helped him regain his composure, and he was no longer crying or shaking.

"We will," I said. "I promise." I wondered how much each individual Brocine had to do with what the pack said. Should I blame Gript for all of them trying to take my calculator?

Gript gave me a nod and jumped down off the bench, disappearing into the crowd.

"Did you understand that?" I asked Becky.

"Not everything, but they said they want you to stay here. You can't!" She pounded a fist on the table, knocking something soft and star-shaped out of her bowl.

"I'm not going to," I said. "But it's not like we can just trick them and run off. The Hottini aren't going to give up, and Front made me promise not to give the calculator to anyone. And what if the Pipe Men really are angry and we do have to escape? We're going to need somebody's help. So I might *have* to trade the calculator to the Brocine. But it won't work without me!" I rubbed my head with my hands in frustration.

"Are you experiencing difficulty in completing your task, Ry-an?" asked Tast-e, smirking. He glared at the Brocine to my left, who scurried aside to let him sit, and stuffed his hind legs comically under the table, pulling his front boots off with his teeth.

"What's your task?" I snapped. "To get me back on your ship and put me in a cell?"

"You should not have made the same bargain with two powerful races," Tast-e observed.

I had nothing to say to that.

22

"**There's nothing on but rat stuff,**" said Becky. She sat on her cot, a makeshift combination of tiny little mattresses, apparently each designed for a single Brocine, and punched the tiny metal screen. The channel changed, but only to another dim view of a wet cave.

"Well, we're on their planet," I said, rolling over. My cot was lumpy, but it was soft enough. After everything I'd been through, I probably could have slept anywhere.

"We get all sorts of stuff at home."

"Ip said there weren't any portals," I said. "We never got any Brocine TV at home either, did we?"

"Thank goodness." She poked a button, and the tiny screen went black.

I sat up on my cot and rubbed my eyes. We were in a warm, dry room aboveground, with a window. Last night it had been too dark to see, but now I saw a wet, lush landscape. Yellow treelike plants with long, dangling limbs hung over red grass and orange bushes. The sky was cloudy, but I could see the tinge of red sky through them. It was nice to see the rain dripping down the outside of the window instead of onto us.

"We don't have time to watch TV anyway," I said. "We have to talk before they come back. You know we're going back to O-thυl-þɑ today, right?"

She nodded.

"Okay, well, I'm not sure where the portal's going to open. I mean, the calcυlɑtor has been used there. Before Front took it from the Pipe Men, and then again when we were running around in the passageway with all the doors. I'm pretty sure I figured out which one it is." I turned the calcυlɑtor on, and the time stamps popped onto the screen. I breathed a sigh of relief. Since it had gotten wet, I hadn't been sure it would keep working. Our food had been completely ruined. I pointed to the times and dates. "See? They're pretty regular, like the Pipe Men were exploring the portals with it. Remember those Pipe Men Ip ran into? So every other one must be O-ᚦʋl-ᚦɑ."

She peered at it from under my arm. "No, those ones are for the passage."

"Well, the passage is on O-ᚦʋl-ᚦɑ."

"No, it isn't."

"What do you mean?"

She rolled her eyes at me. "It's an interdimensional spaceport. It isn't anywhere."

I thought about it. She was right that the passage wasn't on O-ᚦʋl-ᚦɑ. You always had to go through a portal to get there. "But it has to be *some*where," I said.

"Why?"

"Because . . ." I had to think about it. "Because everywhere is *some*where."

"We weren't." She was looking at me solemnly.

"We weren't where?"

"Anywhere. We were in the space between all points."

"Where are you getting this from? Anyway, we had air to breathe. There isn't air in nowhere."

"From Bre-zon-air. I was only supposed to be learning how to add." She rolled her eyes. "He thinks I'm stupid because I don't speak Pipe Man, but I understand the *math*. The air is only as much there as you are."

I knew I was never going to catch up with my little sister on this, and I really didn't care whether the place was anywhere, as long as we could go there. "Well, we have to go back to the passage and find our way to the right door then. I can't be sure which one is O-thʊl-þə just from this."

"You have to know what number to start with," said Becky. "Remember how Front made you put in 44? And *then* you put in 1064? This door will be unknown."

"Unknown?"

"It's like you said—there aren't supposed to be any portals to here. There really is one, but it doesn't have a number yet."

"It isn't there yet," I said. "I'm going to make it."

Becky giggled. "*Ry*-an!"

"What?" I was starting to get frustrated. I just wanted to go there.

"*All* the doors are there. It's the space between *all* places."

"Well, if you're so smart, tell me what number this *already there* door is going be and then tell me what number the zoo is so we can get back there!" I didn't mean to yell, but it came out that way.

Becky sat back down on her cot with a crash and turned the TV on with an angry poke.

"I'm sorry, okay?" I sat down next to her. "I really do need your help."

"I don't know anything," she pouted. "I don't even speak Pipe Man. Nobody tells me what's going on."

"Hey," I tried to put my arm around her, but she flung it off. "I'm sorry. I'll try to translate more. It's just, everything's been happening so fast."

Just then, a trapdoor popped open right next to my feet. A Brocine nose appeared, and then the entire Brocine. I recognized him by the shape of his ears.

"Gript!"

"Sorry to bother you," said Gript, closing the trapdoor with his front paws, "but the suns are rising and . . . oh, my moons." Before I knew what he was doing, he had climbed my leg and was standing on my knee. "The calculator!" He reached out a paw and hesitated reverently without touching it.

I pulled it back.

"Don't worry, Earth," said Gript. "I wouldn't want

to hurt it." He stood still on my leg, staring. His claws dug into my leg.

I squirmed.

"Oh, I am infinitely sorry!" Gript jumped off my leg and landed on the mattress between Becky and me.

"I am infinitely sorry!" said Becky, and grinned at the Brocine. "Would you like some soup?"

"Yes, please and thank you." Gript grinned back, showing his sharp teeth. Before I could say anything, he turned back to me, solemn again. "You must understand, Earth. The calculator is not just a way for me to find my family, or for the Brocine to retrieve their honor from the Masters' zoo. It is a way for us to travel to distant worlds, trade with many people, free of the Masters. The technology inside it will free the universe."

So Gript did agree with the others about stealing the calculator from me. Was there anyone at all I could trust?

I sighed. "Are you sure you don't want to control everything, just like the Masters?" I pictured Front's antennae reaching toward me, his faces solemn as he made me promise not to give the calculator away.

"We will build tunnels to all places. Trade will be free. Kidnapping will be outlawed." Gript flexed his claws, and his ears shook.

"What's he saying?" asked Becky, poking me.

"They want the calculator because then they'll be in control."

"I like him." She patted Gript on the head.

"You liked the Xaxor, too, before it tried to sell us," I said.

Becky glared at me.

Gript turned toward her and flashed his sharp-toothed smile again. His ears stopped shaking quite so much.

A tiny door on the far side of the little room burst open. I had a dim memory of crawling through it the night before, so tired it had been almost torture to put hand in front of knee. They'd said this was one of their "big-quest" rooms. Ten Brocine now poured through the door. They were wearing uniforms, noses pointed straight ahead, each holding in one arm something that looked dangerously like a gun.

"I agreed to do this," I said. "I need this as much as you do."

"They are not here to guard you," said Gript. "They are the rescue mission."

"Only these?" The ten little creatures against all the Pipe Men and their assistants?

"These are the very best. You think we are too small?" He wiggled his barbed nose at me, then waved the Brocine soldiers forward. They came at a march and climbed, one by one, onto the mattress between Becky and me. She smiled at them, but they didn't react. Their noses seemed particularly sharp, their eyes particularly hard.

I waited, but they just stood there.

Gript, at the front of the pack of soldiers, looked up at me and pointed at the calculator. "To O-thul-ba!"

I don't know why I had expected us to go somewhere else, some official launching place, maybe a spaceport, but I had. I hadn't expected to go so soon, with so little fanfare, barely having woken up. I glanced at Becky, everything she'd said about the passage running through my head. I still didn't know which number the portal I was about to make would have. We could get hopelessly lost in the passage, this space between all points, us and a bunch of Brocine, just waiting for the Pipe Men to find us. Or worse, what if nobody found us? I needed time to think about it, work it all out.

"I think the calculator will create a number, once you open the door," said Becky.

"You think?"

"Well, how else do the Pipe Men do it?"

It made sense, but that almost worried me. Making sense wasn't like þok, at least not for me.

"And Ip said that Mom and Dad's closet is 2159. We can go home and then go through our *living room* closet to our zoo sector on O-thʋl-þa."

I almost laughed. We could get there from home! We had a portal right there in our house that went straight to O-thʋl-þa and never changed. As soon as this was all over and we were all safe, I was going to make Becky about a thousand cakes.

Becky tugged on my sleeve. "The cure," she said.

I couldn't believe I had forgotten. "The antidote! Where is it? I'm not doing this without the antidote," I said.

Gript pulled a tiny syringe out of his tiny jacket. It was no bigger than an eyedropper.

"That's going to cure him? Completely?"

Gript put it back in his pocket. "It's worked on every other From."

That had to be good enough. "Okay," I said, reaching for Becky's hand, "you stay with me. No running off into random doors." I turned to Gript. "Give it to me."

"You promise to get us to our people?" Gript stared up at me, eyes beginning to water.

"I promise," I said, and I meant it. No matter what the Brocine pack was planning to do to me, Gript's children didn't deserve to have been kidnapped and forced to live in a zoo sector. I couldn't imagine what it would be like, not being able to go home. "I've never been to the Brocine sector, but I think I can find it."

Gript nodded. "I will be infinitely grateful." He looked into my eyes for a few long seconds, then pulled out the antidote again.

I took it and held it out to Becky. "The Pipe Men aren't going to watch you as closely," I said. "You need to hold on to this, in case they take me away and don't let me see him."

She took it from me and put it in her pocket. Then her eyes started to water and her lip quivered.

"It's going to be fine," I said, squeezing her hand. "It's just in case."

She started to giggle. "Pretty good, huh?"

I couldn't help smiling, but it didn't last long. "You keep it up. You keep it up until they let you see him. If we do get separated, I'll be coming back. I'll find a way to get you all out of there. If we have to escape, it will be all of us. You, me, Mom, and Dad." I tried not to look at Gript and the Brocine soldiers—tried not to think about the fact that they expected me to come back here. Or about where we would really go. I couldn't worry about all that yet.

Becky nodded, solemn again. "I'll tell them. We'll wait for you."

I squeezed Becky's hand, then released it, held the calculator in front of me, and touched the screen.

A black, rectangular portal appeared in front of us. I glanced back at the Brocine.

Gript nodded at me.

I took a step forward.

A whoosh of air came through the portal, and the whole thing expanded as if blown up from the inside. In an instant, it had become the size of the entire wall.

23

THE LIGHT COMING THROUGH the window behind me was now much dimmer. I stopped in my tracks, staring at the giant portal. "What happened?" I said to Becky. If anyone knew what was going on, she did.

"Doggies!"

Several Hottini fell through the portal onto the floor in front of us. Before I could react, the Brocine had fired their weapons. Thin darts shot from the muzzles of the little guns. Several missed, but as there were ten Brocine firing, all of the five Hottini I now counted were hit by something. There were strings attached to the darts, so that the Brocine were connected to their prey.

The Hottini were a mess of legs, clear coverings, and shiny blue hair as they scrambled to right themselves. One tangled with the string from the dart gun and fell back on his haunches with a thud. The others glared at their fallen comrade, until one gingerly offered a leg, and the fallen one pulled himself to standing. They stood there, ignoring the darts attached to various parts of their bodies, glaring at us as if they owned the room.

The Brocine soldiers jumped off the mattress and re-formed their pyramid directly in front of the Hottini. Gript stayed behind on the mattress.

"Declare your purpose," said one of the Brocine soldiers, at the front of the formation.

"The Earth child has what is ours," said the Hottini in the middle, fixing his purple eyes on the calculator in my hand.

"How did you get here?" I asked.

Just then, a Hottini head appeared in the middle of the wall behind the others. It was Grav-e. He glared at me before barking something in their language.

Two of the other Hottini turned to go back through the giant portal, but they were caught short by the darts from the Brocine soldiers, who still stood stiffly in formation. I couldn't figure out how something so small could hold something so big. The Brocine didn't seem to be straining at all.

"Let them go," said Grav-e.

"You invaded our system! How did you get here?" shouted the Brocine leader.

"You stole our prisoner," said Grav-e, ignoring the question.

"I'm cold," said Becky.

As soon as she said it, I realized I was cold, too.

Becky was actually starting to shiver.

The trapdoor that Gript had come through burst all the way open, and a stream of Brocine jumped into the room, chattering loudly in their language.

Grav-e said something I couldn't understand, and then the other Hottini began barking.

"Stop it! You're hurting my ears. Stop!" yelled Becky.

No one stopped.

I waved the calculator, and it shook even more than I intended, because now I was really shivering. "You all want this!"

That did something. The Brocine pulled together in a pack, the soldiers rising to the top, still holding their weapons. The Hottini also moved closer together, leaving a space in the center for Grav-e's head.

"I'm cold!" Becky yelled into the sudden silence.

The Brocine pack turned toward her as one. For the

first time, I noticed that their hairs were standing up, and many of them appeared to be shivering too.

"IF anybody wants this, you're going to have to tell me what's going on!" I cried, waving the calculator. In the silence, my voice was louder than it needed to be, but at least all eyes were on me now.

"We are farther from the suns," said the pack, in its deep voice.

Gript, who was still with Becky, separate from the pack, squeaked.

I turned and pressed my face up against the window. It was darker outside, sure, and the suns had only just risen, but . . . it couldn't be true.

"And you must tell us what you have done," said the pack, turning back to the Hottini.

"It was hot underground," said Becky. She crawled to the trapdoor the Brocine had come through. It appeared to be just big enough for a person to squeeze through.

"Becky, we don't know where it goes," I said. But she was already stuffing herself into it. I grabbed my backpack from the remains of my mattress and jammed the calculator into it. Before I had finished, she was gone.

Gript squeaked and jumped after her.

I glanced back at the Brocine and the Hottini.

"Stop!" The Brocine pack leaned menacingly toward me. Then they jerked backward. The Hottini were pulling them by their own darts. The pack fell apart into its Brocine pieces as the soldiers were pulled, screeching, through the portal behind the disappearing Hottini.

I jumped into the hole and found I was still in the room from the waist up. I wriggled my legs into the tunnel below and squeezed myself downward, until I was on all fours. The tunnel was about the same size as the one we'd originally come through. Brocine dropped on either side of me. They scampered past me farther into the tunnel, where Becky and Gript were waiting. Becky was on her hands and knees, looking backward toward me, and Gript was standing behind her, waving frantically at me with one paw. I pulled the trapdoor shut and crawled forward.

"Move," said Gript to Becky. She seemed to understand and crawled forward over the cold, damp ground. The rest of the Brocine pack was now long gone, but Gript stayed with us as we slowly and painfully crawled down the dark tunnel. Out of some tiny pocket, he had pulled out a light no bigger than the dropper with my father's cure. It shone a soft red color.

"Gript, do you have any idea what happened?"

"Obviously the Hottini interfered with your portal somehow. I did not know they had the capacity to do that."

"Not the portal, the planet! How could it move?"

"How should I know? I sell spices for soup!"

"In a spaceship!"

"I don't know!" Gript squealed. The paw holding the light was definitely shaking, and it wasn't nearly as cold down here.

"It's okay, I just . . . We have to move the planet back!" I was trying not to freak out, but it wasn't working. Farther from the *suns?*

"The doggies are dumb," said Becky.

"Yeah, so dumb they figured out how to open a portal as big as a wall and stop us from getting to O-thul-ba," I snapped.

"You're dumb too. Front should have given the calculator to me."

She was probably right. We crawled on in silence for a few long minutes.

"I think they ripped something they shouldn't have," Becky finally said.

"What do you mean?"

"I mean, the big portal. Portals aren't supposed to move planets. They tried to change where your portal was going, and it did something bad."

"Becky thinks the Hottini tried to hijack my portal and messed up," I translated for Gript. "But how could they?" I repeated it in English.

"Tast-e went with us on purpose," said Becky. "So they could track what planet we went to."

"It's probably related to the probes they've been placing in our system," said Gript. "They send new ones as fast as we can take them down. We had no idea they were far enough along with bok to attempt this."

Suddenly, it hit me out of nowhere. "Gript, do you know where they took the Xaxor?" The Hottini wanted the Xaxor back, too. The Brocine weren't going to make protecting it a priority. What if the Hottini got to it and took it away before I could help it? What if they ruined everything, and I could never open another portal? What if we all froze to death because we were *too far from the suns*? I missed something Gript said.

"What?" I gasped. "What did you say?"

Gript stopped in his tracks and stared at me.

"You're talking English," said Becky.

I stopped crawling and closed my eyes. I had to get it together. It was still warm enough down here. We weren't going to die. We were going to follow the other Brocine, and find the Xaxor, and fix this problem with the planet, and get back to O-thʊl-ᵬᵅ, and save Gript's family, and get to my dad, and . . . I couldn't take it. It was too much to do, too many impossible hurdles.

"Ryan, come on." I heard Becky's voice, but it seemed to be coming from far away. I didn't want to open my eyes. "Ryan." I opened them to find her peering into my face. Gript was standing between us, shining the light up into my face. "Ryan, there's a hole going down. Ask him if it's the way to go."

"Earth?" said Gript.

"Earth to Ryan," said Becky.

"Do we go down it?" I asked, taking a deep breath. My hands were shaking so much, I wasn't sure if they were going to keep holding me up.

"Yes, yes," said Gript. "The pack will be down there."

"Okay. Let's go," I said.

At the bottom of the hole was not another tunnel, but a cavern. Where we stood, the ceiling was just above my head, but it gradually got higher until it was nearly as big as the first one we'd been in the day before. A pack of Brocine were squished together at the center, so tightly I couldn't distinguish any individual features. They were facing a giant, gaping black portal that seemed to be cutting through the entire cave. Whatever the Hottini had made, it was a lot bigger than the room we'd just been in. The portal was to my left, and the Brocine were to my right. On the far side of the pack, guarded by a group of soldiers, stood Tast-e. His covering was gone, and his hair was matted together in clumps. One ear hung limply to the side. But he stood up straight as he glared in our direction.

On the side of the pack closest to us, unguarded and sitting on the floor, was the Xaxor. It jumped up and scurried lightly over. It seemed to have fully recovered from the water, and it was even walking on its injured leg. Its three eyes opened wide at me, and it blinked furiously in a pattern I couldn't understand.

The ten Brocine soldiers came through the giant portal, pulling the five Hottini along behind them by their darts. The Brocine were grinning their toothy grins, apparently quite satisfied to have gotten the upper hand again. Grav-e followed out of the portal, surveying the scene calmly. He wasn't being pulled by any Brocine, and he didn't even look at his ignominiously captured soldiers.

The Brocine soldiers and the pack had a furious conversation in their language, with much squeaking and many high-pitched growls. Then they all suddenly stopped, and the main pack all stared pointedly at Grav-e, who serenely stepped forward past the soldiers.

"It seems our home planets have been sucked together by the creation of the portal," said Grav-e.

"Your portal," I said, stepping forward. "You did this."

Grav-e regarded me regally.

"So you undo it," I said. "Undo whatever you did, or we're all going to freeze to death."

"You freeze," said Grav-e. "We burn." He turned to the pack. "Your two suns have added to our one."

"Wait a minute, your planet is here?" I asked.

"Our planet is not here," Grav-e said witheringly, still speaking to the pack. "The distance between us has been displaced, causing your suns to radiate heat to our system."

"If there's an extra sun, why are we freezing?" I asked.

"The portal has moved you away from all of them."

"But how can . . . ? Whatever. Just fix it!" I crossed my arms and glared right back at Grav-e.

Grav-e's eyes flicked almost imperceptibly from side to side.

"You don't know how to fix it."

Grav-e lifted his head and shoulders up even higher and stared past me. "This is the first time we have had occasion to interfere with a portal."

The Brocine burst into excited chatter. The soldiers stopped in unison and gave a sharp tug at their darts, pulling the Hottini awkwardly forward. Since the darts were attached to various body parts, the Hottini ended up sprawled in different positions. Boots thumped and scraped as the startled Hottini attempted to right themselves. The soldiers tugged, and the Hottini were dragged toward the pack, leaving Grav-e and me behind.

"Unhand my soldiers!" Grav-e boomed.

"Undo what you did," the pack boomed back.

"We have more soldiers. Shall I call them?"

Something zipped past us near the floor. Grav-e slowly looked down. I followed his gaze and saw that a dart had lodged in Grav-e's leg. At the other end, Gript stood, grinning with all his teeth.

"I'd rather you stayed," said Gript.

"Wait!" I jumped between Grav-e and Gript, careful not to trip over the line between them. I knew if Gript jerked Grav-e around like they'd done to the others, we'd never get any help getting the portal closed. "The Hottini don't know how to close the portal." I looked pointedly at Grav-e, whose eyes focused on the ceiling. "But they want it closed too. Let's sit down and talk about it."

Everyone was silent for a minute. The pack sat completely still, but its various eyes moved, taking in the positions of the Hottini sprawled around the cave.

"Fine," said the pack. "We'll sit. Let them move freely, and release the leader."

The Hottini raised themselves to their feet and, as calmly as possible, sat down on their haunches. Gript glared at me for a second, but he released the dart from Grav-e with a pop. Carefully, Grav-e sat. Tast-e made a move to come forward and join his comrades, but Brocine closed in around him.

"Not him." The pack pointed their collective noses at Tast-e as they spoke. "This one is a spy. We will deal with him later."

Tast-e sat down with a controlled thump, still behind his Brocine guards. Even sitting on their haunches, the Hottini managed to look regal and in control. But the Brocine looked fierce, with their weaponized noses and the sharp teeth that flashed as they talked excitedly with each other.

"Go out there," said Becky, pointing to the center of the cave, between the main Brocine pack and the Hottini. "You have to, or they'll kill each other."

The Xaxor blinked at me. I could have sworn it was saying the same thing.

"Okay. Listen to me." I looked from the Hottini to the Brocine, ready to race between them.

A sizzling, cracking noise filled the cave, making me jump. The Hottini all looked up and around, and the Brocine started to chatter. It was clear that no one else had expected this, either. I turned around to find Gript scurrying past me to the far side of the cave. The pack turned as one to follow him, then squeaked something.

Gript stood up on his hind legs and poked the wall with his nose. With a quiet scraping, a section of wall slid upward into the ceiling, revealing a TV screen about as tall as I was.

On the screen appeared a single Pipe Man, in a small room that was empty except for the Pipe Man and a row of assistant wires. It looked out at us with sixteen many-shaded purple eyes.

"Hon-tri-bum," I said.

Gript scurried back over to me, opening his yellow eyes wide. "You know the Minister of Trade?"

"It used to visit me in the zoo. Can it see us?"

Gript turned back to the screen. "Yes. The screen is for internal communications between our planets. I don't know how the Masters are using it."

Hon-tri-bum turned three of its eyes toward me, pointing the rest at the Brocine, the Hottini, the Xaxor, and Becky. "Ry-an, the Earth child?" Hon-tri-bum's mouth opened in an O. It was the first time I'd seen Hon-tri-bum surprised.

Without really thinking about it, I raised my arms up, brought them down quickly, and bowed deeply.

Hon-tri-bum turned half of its eyes to Grav-e. "You

have torn a rift of variable infinity, and you have also stolen our prized specimens?" Two eyes flitted to Becky and me.

I raised my arms. "We're fine," I said, "but—"

Grav-e cut me off. "You have no right to hoard bok or these specimens. We stole them right from your planet. If you don't go away, we'll cut a portal right next to O-thul-ba and push the whole planet in."

"My eyes are vibrating in fear," said Hon-tri-bum.

I was about to say something, but Becky poked me in the side and gave me a pointed look. The Xaxor had come with her and was blinking furiously again. They were right. It was definitely better for the Pipe Men to think the Hottini had stolen us than for them to know we'd run away. We might even be able to go back if we wanted to.

"The Hottini said they were going to sell us," I said.

The Xaxor shrank a little. It knew how I'd come up with that lie.

The movement caught Hon-tri-bum's attention. "A Xaxor? I'm not surprised to find the swarm involved in this. Strange creatures. What do they need all the legs for?" Hon-tri-bum squinted its top two eyes in laughter.

"Strange? It should talk," said Becky.

I tried not to laugh myself.

"This Xaxor tried to steal our specimens," said Grav-e, ignoring the fact that he'd just claimed to have stolen us first. "It's ours, and I'll thank you not to interfere."

"Thieves of the known universe," said Hon-tribum. "Its swarm just stiffed the Yum-Yoms for a very expensive batch of Yim. Don't get mixed up with them, Ry-an. And if the Hottini ever release you," he said to the Xaxor, pointing three eyes, "tell your swarm they are not welcome at any O-thul-ban spaceport until they pay the treble restitution."

"What's Yim?" Becky whispered.

"I think it's some kind of candy. Sweet drink?" I asked the Xaxor.

The Xaxor nodded its top section and wilted a little more.

"How do they eat it without a mouth?" asked Becky.

While we'd been talking, the Brocine pack had been quietly conferring among themselves. As one, they turned their noses toward the screen.

"These warmongering Hottini have opened a rift

they don't know how to close," said the pack. "We would thank the honored Masters for their generous assistance."

Hon-tri-bum pointed all sixteen eyes at the Brocine pack, then shifted them all to Grav-e and his soldiers. "Tell me," he said, "why are the Hottini here in the first place?"

No one was going to admit that they were fighting over a calculator stolen from the Pipe Men. Not being able to confer about the best lie to tell, Grav-e and the pack remained silent while Hon-tri-bum shifted various eyes from one group to the other.

I realized that no one was paying attention to us, and I knew what we had to do. I quietly took Becky's hand. "We're going to run past Grav-e, into the rift, okay?"

She nodded.

"Follow us," I whispered to Gript and the Xaxor.

"In there? We don't know where it goes," whispered Gript.

"Do you want to save your family?" I whispered.

Hon-tri-bum was still glaring back and forth between the pack and the Hottini.

Gript glanced quickly at his pack, who appeared to take no notice of him, then nodded at me.

"Now." I ran past Grav-e, pulling Becky. It only took a few seconds to reach the rift, and I didn't look back. I kept running right through. Right into something hard.

"Ow!" Becky had hit it, too.

Gript knocked into my leg.

"You're on me again!" Becky cried.

That accounted for the Xaxor.

I looked down to make sure I didn't kick Gript, who had now made it to one side of me. Then I took a small step backward. I was staring at something smooth and metal. It seemed about twice as tall as me, and to my left and right, it curved away, as if we were outside of a great cylinder. There was enough room to walk between the cylinder and the wall, but only just. Behind us, the wall was moving slightly, meaning the rift was still as open as ever.

"Come on," I said. "We have to move before they decide to come after us."

Nobody needed a translation. Gript was already walking down the passage, on two legs, claws up. The floor was made of something like wood and gave a little under our steps. On our left, the portal was still there, its blackness swirling as we turned in a circle, and the cylinder opened up to reveal a round room, in the middle of which two Hottini in black coverings like Grav-e's stood in front of a panel of glowing instruments. Behind the Hottini, a passage several feet wide led up into darkness.

Before I had a chance to do anything, Gript lifted his dart gun and shot both of the Hottini.

"Don't move or I'll pull you through the portal," said Gript. "It didn't work out so well for your friends."

The Hottini barked at each other for a few seconds. One pointed to something on the display with a bootless, fingered foot. The other attempted to step backward, but seemed unable to move more than an inch. He shook the leg in which the dart was lodged as if trying to shake off a fly.

"How do those darts work?" I asked.

Gript showed his teeth to the immobilized Hottini. "Larger objects create a certain force. The dart directs that force along the line back to the weapon. So the stronger the victim, the easier it is to hold."

Becky poked me.

"He said the dart works by using the bigger victim's force against him."

"What if we used it on the Brocine? I mean, we're bigger than them," she said.

I didn't quite want to ask Gript that question, so I just shrugged.

"What is this place?" asked Gript.

The Hottini looked at each other for a few seconds. Then one spoke. "Experimental bok lab."

"Close the portal," said Gript.

"We have tried," said the same Hottini. He tugged at the dart planted in his leg, but it wouldn't budge.

"Open one now, because they're coming," said Becky.

She was right. I heard footsteps somewhere. I pulled out the calculator.

"No!" shouted the two Hottini together.

"Why not?" I asked, holding my hand next to the place I rubbed to turn it on.

"It will make the rupture worse! We designed this to latch on whenever that device creates a portal anywhere within a thousand-light-year range of any of our sensors," said the one on the left. It stared at me with earnest light purple eyes. "There's a sensor right here in this room!"

The footsteps were getting louder. It sounded like a whole company of heavy-booted Hottini soldiers.

"We have to get out of here, and we're not going back," I said. "If you don't want me to use this"—I waved the calculator in the air—"you're going to have to get us a thousand light years away!"

Two Hottini heads appeared in the passage. Though it was dark behind them, I saw the outline of more. They barked at the two at the controls. The two at the controls barked back, waving their tethered legs and pointing at Gript and me. All pointed several times at the calculator, which I held up, showing I was ready to use it.

Finally, the controller on the left turned back to me. "We will give you a ship."

"They say they'll give us a ship," I said to Becky.

"It's a trick," she said.

The Xaxor put its tablet in front of me. It's a trick, it read.

"I know," I said to Becky, "but what happens if I try it here? We won't get anywhere, and we'll just make things worse."

"Okay," I said to the Hottini, "but we're keeping these two until we get on safely." I looked pointedly at Gript, and he nodded, teeth bared.

Becky and the Xaxor eyed each other, then me.

"I know, but what else can we do?"

Becky shrugged.

"Okay, then, let's go." I took Becky's hand and led the way past the Hottini controllers.

The ones in the passage had turned and were clomping their way back up, all except for the two in front. They glared at me coldly, but as soon as I got near them, they also turned and began clomping up.

Becky and I followed them into the darkness, walking up a smooth slope. The Xaxor followed us, and Gript came last, towing the Hottini controllers, who barked at each other quietly in their language. I didn't like that at all, but I tried to put it out of my mind. There was no point in worrying about what they were saying, because it wouldn't change anything.

The passage went up and up and up, and before long, it began to turn inward and spiral. I was starting to sweat.

"I'm hot," said Becky.

"Me too," I said. Both of our hands were sweating

so much that it was hard to hang on to each other. "I wonder if it's because of the portal." Supposedly, the Hottini planet was now too hot because it was too close to the Brocine suns. I still didn't understand how that could be, but I couldn't deny how I was feeling. I turned around and saw that the Xaxor was laboring, Gript had sweat dripping off his fur, and the Hottini controllers had shaken off their coverings, exposing matted, dripping blue hair. The Hottini who had been leading us were now too far ahead to see.

"I want to sit," said Becky. She pulled against my hand, but I lifted her up again.

"We're almost there," I said. "Look." There was a light ahead of us, and the outlines of the leaders' backsides were just visible. Their tails were sticking up, and as we got closer, I saw that they had shaken their coverings off, too. My clothes were so stuck to me with sweat, I wasn't sure if I could have gotten them off. When we reached the Hottini leaders, they stepped forward, allowing us to come out of the tunnel and into the sun — or suns.

We were in a brilliant meadow. Everything was bright Technicolor green, contrasting strangely, yet in a way that appeared perfectly natural somehow, with the bright blue of the Hottini manes. There were grasslike things, some with flowers of a deeper green, and thin trees with wild, thick green plumage on top. There were smooth metallic paths through the meadow, leading out into the distance, where miles away, a brilliant blue metallic city rose out of the ground. But there was something wrong with the green plants. All of them seemed to be wilting, falling over on themselves.

The sun was so bright that I had to hold my hand over my eyes, but I could see a wall of black surrounding the metallic dome we had just come out of. The structure went only about ten eyes above our heads, but above the top of the dome, the rift rose far up into the air. The blackness blocked out everything behind it.

"Ask them if they have water," Becky croaked.

I was thirsty, too, but before I could ask, a grinding filled all the space for sound. In front of us, maybe fifty yards out, the paths broke and shifted, and a hole opened up in the ground, widening slowly into a gaping circle. Out of the hole, a platform emerged, lifting a structure up. It was round and nondescript, only the size of my bedroom at home, and dull amid the shininess of the paths and the city in the background. Dents riddled its hull.

Becky tugged on my shirt.

"Do you have water?" I asked.

One of the Hottini lifted its booted foot and pointed at the structure that had risen out of the ground. "The ship has supplies."

"That's our ship?" I exchanged disbelieving looks with Gript.

The Xaxor hummed and stared at the ship with all three eyes.

"It will go one thousand light years," said the Hottini.

"Wait a minute. I don't know much about spaceships," I said, "but one thousand light years sounds like a long way. Are you sure that old thing can make it?"

"You want us to give away our best ship?" the Hottini snapped, letting his boot fall with a thump.

The Xaxor typed furiously on its tablet. If this is the Hottini home planet, then there is a tunnel that will take us about 800 light years. We will need to travel only a few hours to a tunnel that will take us 400 more.

I was pretty sure that the Xaxor hadn't mentioned those tunnels when we were making the map. But now wasn't the time to point that out. I showed the tablet to Gript. "It says it knows how to get far enough and we only have to go a few hours in this thing," I said to Becky.

"It knows," said Becky, rolling her eyes. "It's probably going to try to sell us again."

"Well, they said there's water on the ship."

She scrunched up her face.

"Look, we don't have to trust the Xaxor or the ship, okay?" I certainly didn't trust the ship, but the Xaxor? I *thought* it was sorry. "We'll just open a portal the second we're far enough away. We'll be back on O-thʋl-þa. You still have the antidote, right?"

She nodded.

"Okay. See? Everything's going to be fine." I tried not to look at the ship. Sweat was still dripping off me in buckets. The plants were looking even more wilted than they had a minute ago. I was starting to think that we'd better take any chance to get off this planet. "Let's go."

The ship's door fell open with a clang, revealing a ramp studded with reassuringly solid-looking treads. We all headed toward it, Gript bringing up the rear, towing the two reluctant Hottini, who attempted to look as haughty as possible while being jerked along by tiny darts. As soon as we got to the ramp, the Xaxor scampered up it, waiting for us near the top. I pushed Becky in front of me and followed partway, waiting for Gript.

"I am infinitely sorry," said Gript, bowing a little, and he released the two Hottini. The dart gun popped as it sucked the darts back up into the tube.

Everything happened at once. Becky fell toward me, pushed by a single Hottini who appeared through the ship's hatch. The Xaxor jumped on the Hottini, who tried to buck the Xaxor off. I caught Becky, but she threw me off balance, and we both went tumbling down the ramp. Gript was screaming something, but I couldn't see him.

25

I ROLLED THIS WAY AND THAT, reaching for Becky but not finding her. Finally I scrambled to my feet, trying to get my bearings, and found I was facing back toward the dome. The rift was now lined with Pipe Men. They were mostly facing it. Some held calculators like mine in their top-holes, while others were using their top-holes to roll assistant wires out of the rift. Others held pens and were poking calculators held by their comrades.

I stuffed my calculator into my bag, out of their sight. I had no idea if they cared enough to "rescue" us from the Hottini, and I didn't want to wait to find out. I turned toward the ship, just in time to see Becky and the Xaxor push an unconscious Hottini out of the hatch.

They pushed him hard enough that he missed the ramp entirely and fell to the ground with a thud.

"Come on, Ryan!" Becky yelled, waving frantically at me.

"Where's Gript?" I looked around, and finally I saw him. The two Hottini controllers, whom Gript had recently held hostage with his darts, were now holding him between their boots. It did not take two Hottini to hold one Brocine, but they appeared to be enjoying themselves, squeezing him and whispering into his twitching ears. Gript's nose twitched too. The other Hottini had retreated back toward the dome and were engaged in a heated conversation with two Pipe Men, one of whom was pointing at least some of its eyes in my direction.

"Put it down," I said.

The two Hottini stopped whispering to Gript and looked at me. "You want it?" said one.

"Ryan, come on!" yelled Becky.

Both of the Pipe Men were looking my direction now.

I walked up to the Hottini and grabbed Gript, tearing him from their grasp.

I held poor Gript with his back flat against my chest

as I ran up the ramp toward Becky. As soon as I got to the top, the hatch slammed shut. The shock tossed me to the ground.

Gript squealed and rolled off me.

"I'm sorry," I gasped. "I didn't know what else to do."

"How do we know this ship will even fly?" Gript asked. "Clearly they never intended to let us take it."

For answer, the ship began to groan. I stumbled to my feet, holding on to a bulkhead for support, and saw the Xaxor at the controls. One of its legs was wrapped around a lever, another poked at a series of buttons, and a third waved wildly at Becky, who was pushing on another lever with both hands, her face red and scrunched with effort. I ran to help her, and together, we pushed the lever up until it caught in the top of a dashboard full of seemingly random screens and incomprehensible symbols.

The whole ship was shaking, and it felt like it was lifting, but there were no windows, so there was no way to see for sure how far we'd gone. There was a crackling, and then a voice filled the cabin.

"This is Hottini Space Control. Set down immediately, or we will shoot you down."

"The Masters won't like it if you kill their prized specimens," Gript shouted.

"I don't think they can hear you," I said, hoping the Hottini would think of that anyway.

The Xaxor turned its eyes toward me, one leg hovering over a button, another reaching up to wrap around a lever planted in the ceiling just above its head. It pointed to the lever Becky and I had just pushed up and then to another one next to it, making a pushing motion.

"You want us to push this one up now?"

The Xaxor nodded.

"This is your final warning," said the Hottini voice.

"Now!" I shouted.

Becky and I pushed the lever. The Xaxor pulled on the lever above its head and pounded the button. The ship shot unmistakably upward. My stomach went the other way. Becky let go of the lever, doubled over, and threw up on my boots. Gript hung on to her ankle with both front paws.

I hung on to the lever, and it was all I could do to hold it up. I looked over at the Xaxor to see if I could stop, but it was still clinging to its lever and pushing its button, balancing on taut legs as if it were having trouble, too. This went on for what seemed like several minutes, but may only have been thirty seconds or so, until the Xaxor suddenly let go, wrapped a leg around my arm, and pulled me off the lever. The ship shook violently, and I stumbled and almost tripped over Becky, but caught myself on a pole running from floor to ceiling.

The Xaxor moved to where I'd been and began furiously pushing buttons, watching sparks of light that moved along the dashboard. The ship stopped shaking and now felt too still. Becky and Gript both managed to get to standing, and the Xaxor, no longer pushing buttons, stared at the dashboard, legs taut.

The ship jerked again, and the Xaxor kept watching the dashboard.

"Did we go through a tunnel?" I asked. "Are we far enough away yet?"

The Xaxor held up one leg toward me and shook its top section. I remembered what it had said before, about having to go through two tunnels.

"Is this ship going to make it?" The ship was shaking a little but seemed to be holding steady. It was disorienting, not having a window to look out of, not being able to tell anything about where we were or where we were going.

"The Xaxor said it would take a few hours," said Becky. "I'm going to find the water." She began walking around the cabin, poking whatever looked like it might be a door or a cabinet.

"Do you think they'll come after us?" I whispered to Gript. I pulled yesterday's socks out of my backpack and tried to wipe my boots clean.

Gript wiggled his nose and shook his head. "We have to hope they're too busy worrying about their planet." He let out a squeaky laugh. "They thought they were going to get bok, but they ended up crawling to the Masters for help!"

I tried to smile. It was nice to see those superior Froms put in their place, but I was too nervous to be happy about it. Then I thought of something. "Why don't the Hottini and the Brocine work together instead of fighting over me? You could both have bok already."

"I wonder that we can even sell each other spice," said Gript. "Look at us. We're as different as a cave and a sunspot." He saw my confused expression. "It's a saying we have. Our ancestors believed we were descended from gods who came from the large sun. They found the sun too hot and dry, so they traveled to Brock and lived underground in cool, wet caves. They decided they were now too cold and wet, but by then they had lost their immortality and forgotten how to return to the sun."

I wondered if my people, Earth people, had a myth like that. I thought it was something I should know, that I must have heard it somewhere, but I couldn't think what it might be. It bothered me, that I didn't know anything about my own people. Now I might never learn anything.

"What I mean," said Gript, "is that all the Froms I've seen are so different." He gestured at the Xaxor, still watching the controls. "Six legs, three eyes, no mouth. You who are big think we who are small are a joke. If not for our spaceships and our weapons, we would be gone. The Masters think all of us are deficient. Primitive, with our limbs and teeth."

"Aha!" Becky appeared from under a ledge holding a square container with what looked like a straw sticking out of it. She shook the container, and it sloshed. Before I could stop her, she was sucking on the straw.

"Becky!" I held my breath.

She grinned. "Water!"

"What if it was rocket fuel or something?"

"There'd be cross-eyes. Probably on a doggie head."

She handed the container to me.

I wanted to be mad, but I was too thirsty. I didn't even realize how thirsty until I started drinking. It was all I could do to stop drinking and give some to Gript. He drank, and we brought it over to the Xaxor, who dipped two of its legs into the container, humming contentedly with the other four.

The Xaxor peered carefully at all the gauges, then left the controls and sat down with us in the middle of the floor. Becky pulled another canister of water out from under the ledge, along with a box full of wafers wrapped in Pipe Man fabric. They were dull and tasteless but better than nothing.

The ship hummed and shook as it moved, but it generally seemed to be holding together. Becky ate a little bit, then lay down on the floor. The Xaxor had its eyes closed too, its legs folded completely under it. Only Gript seemed to be wide awake, gnawing nervously on his paws.

"What's wrong?" I whispered.

"How am I going to rescue my family without the soldiers? I don't even have my weapon anymore!"

"I've been thinking about that," I said. Something had been in the back of my mind, percolating ever since we'd run from the cave. "The Masters think the Hottini came to O-thul-ba and stole us. That might mean we can just go back, pretend we're happy to be there. I can find your family and rescue them without having to fight at all."

Gript kept chewing on his paws.

"You're small enough to hide in my backpack. We'll figure something out."

"I hope they're all right." Gript wrapped his paws around his chest. His golden eyes began to water.

"They are," I said, thinking about my dad, how he looked lying there with all the wires over him. I wondered if he was still alive.

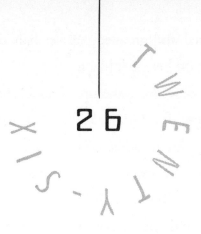

26

I OPENED MY EYES. Everything was blurry. I blinked, trying to see, trying to remember what was going on. My head was touching something cold and hard. I tried to lift it, but it was too heavy. I groaned. A few minutes went by, and I tried again to lift my head. This time, it worked a little better. My eyes were starting to clear, showing me something metallic, shiny. The ceiling of the spaceship. In a flash, my mind came back to me. I sat up slowly, aching all over. My arms and legs tingled like I'd been lying on them funny. My neck itched, and I ran my hand over a welt the size of a nickel.

Becky was lying on her side in front of me. Her arm was stretched out beneath her head. It wasn't how she normally slept.

"Becky?" I crawled over to her, shook her gently.

She shifted and groaned. As her hair moved, it revealed a welt on her neck like mine.

"Becky, come on, wake up." I shook her again and looked around for Gript. I almost screamed, but it caught in my throat. A hatch was open next to the ship's controls, and just inside it was a Xaxor. It was not our Xaxor, but a different one. It looked exactly the same as ours, but I could tell. Its eyes glared at me, without any friendship. Behind it, four more Xaxor perched on their bug legs.

As I stared at the scene, trying to make sense of it, Becky managed to sit up. She took it in silently.

"He stole us again," she said.

The Xaxor at the front of the line stepped into the room. The other four scurried behind it, making a row between us and the controls. The very last one of these was our Xaxor. Somehow, I'd learned to tell it apart from the others. Maybe it was the way it wilted a little, the guilty bug.

I looked away from it and talked to the first one. "What are you going to do now, sell us?"

"They didn't come for you," said Gript, pushing his way between two of the Xaxor.

"Then what?" I asked, but before the words were

out, I realized what he was talking about. "The calculator."

Becky grabbed my backpack and stuck her hand inside. "It's gone," she said, glaring lasers at the row of bugs.

The first Xaxor in the row held up the calculator in one leg. But it looked different than it had before. It was now wrapped in what looked like pieces of Xaxor legs, leaving just enough space for some light to spill out from the screen.

"They figured out how to use it," said Gript, running forward to meet me. None of the Xaxor tried to stop him. "I saw them open a portal while I was hiding under the controls." He turned back to the row of Xaxor and shook his nose. "You can't poison a Brocine."

I rubbed the sore spot on my neck. How was this possible? It was supposed to only work for me. Front was going to be so mad. And now I was never going to get home. I was never going to get the antidote to Dad.

Our Xaxor stepped forward, pulling his tablet out of his pouch.

They have agreed not to sell you. We will open a portal to the passage, and you will be free to go.

"So that makes you our friend now?" I snapped.

"You're not going to sell us? You might as well. We need the calculator to find the right door. We might need it to escape forever. You know that."

The Xaxor wilted even more and pointed all three eyes at its tablet, as if it couldn't think of what to say.

Becky poked me.

"They're not going to sell us, but they're going to keep the calculator." I sighed. "I don't know what to do."

"Ask them to help," Gript whispered.

"Why would they help us?" The twelve eyes of the four unknown Xaxor glared at us. There was nothing friendly about them.

"It feels guilty," said Gript, pointing to our Xaxor.

As Gript talked, it folded up its legs and lowered itself to the ground, head hanging over its middle section.

"You could at least come with us to the hospital so we can save our parent. You have the most powerful technology in the universe because of us. We trusted you!" I shouted the last part. At that moment, the Xaxor didn't seem so scary. They weren't going to hurt us. They were just a bunch of bugs.

Our Xaxor lifted its body up a little, then turned its eyes toward the one next to it. That one began rubbing its legs, causing a shrill humming. Soon, the others joined in.

"They're actually considering it," Gript whispered.

I reached out for Becky's hand, barely daring to breathe.

Finally, after a lot more humming, the one our Xaxor had turned to, who seemed to be the leader, skittered forward and took the tablet from our Xaxor.

You have helped one of us; therefore, we will help you.

The four unknown Xaxor stepped into the portal first, taking the calculator with them. It didn't look like my calculator anymore, still wrapped in what seemed to be parts of Xaxor legs, so that the screen was almost invisible. But the Xaxor apparently didn't need to see the screen. The one who carried it held it close to its chest, two legs wrapped all around it. I wondered what Front would think if he knew that the Xaxor not only had the calculator, but had somehow figured out how to use it without me. Were they as bad as the Hottini and the Brocine, or were they worse?

"You first," said Gript. He was riding in my backpack, claws on my shoulders, nose perilously close to my neck.

I shifted my head a little.

"Don't worry, Earth. I've got my nose under control." He gave a squeaky chuckle. "Only babies poke people without meaning to."

Becky giggled. "Babies." It sounded like "hic-hic" in English.

"Okay, okay. Once we go back in the passage, we have to be serious. We're going straight to our house. No stops anywhere, no matter what happens. If the Pipe Men come out, we act like we were kidnapped by the Hottini and the Xaxor rescued us."

"I know." She rolled her eyes.

"Gript?" I repeated it in Pipe Man.

"I got it. I'm not here." With that, Gript slid down into the backpack. I swung it around and closed the zipper over his head.

"Can he breathe?" Becky asked.

"I left it a little open, see? It's open, so you can't make any noise."

Gript wiggled his nose at me. I hoped that was the Brocine version of a thumbs-up.

Our Xaxor pointed a leg toward the portal, indicating for us to go first.

"You don't trust us?" I couldn't forgive it for stealing my calculator, for knocking us out, and for letting the Xaxor board our ship. It didn't have to do that. If it was really our friend, it would have helped us get away.

The Xaxor let all of its eyes rest on me, then pointed two eyes and a second leg toward the portal.

"Fine." I stepped into the passage, pulling Becky. I didn't see the other Xaxor at first. All I saw was the passageway, how different it looked. The walls were not the same pinkish color, but had changed to many shades of pink and red, darker in some places than in others. And there were black splotches, misshapen and unevenly spaced along the bottom of the doors. The doors were barely recognizable — swirling pockets of black and red, no longer square, churning in different directions from each other. Even the walls were not clearly walls, blending into the floor and ceiling so that the whole passage was like a disfigured tube.

"Bless my eyes," I said.

"The floor is squooshy," said Becky. She scratched her ear. "It's doing something."

The Xaxor, seeing that we had come through, began skittering along, apparently unconcerned. It made sense, since they had never been here before. They wouldn't know it had changed.

My steps were heavy, as if I were sinking into wet earth. If I hadn't looked down and seen fleshy pinkness, I would have thought I was walking through a bog. I wished I were like the Xaxor, who went so lightly that they never sank in even an inch.

"Is the air in here different, too?" I asked.

"It's hot," said Becky. She was sweating, and my tunic was sticking to me again.

"I hope whatever changed the passage didn't change the way the doors are numbered."

"It didn't," said Becky.

"How can you tell?"

"They make my ears pop. Can't you feel them?" She tapped her left ear. "They go duh-dum, duh-dum. It stings."

I concentrated, but I couldn't hear or feel anything.

We followed the four Xaxor around a bend to the left, then a bend to the right, then down a long curving passage that grew hotter and darker as we went.

"Do you think we're getting close?" I asked.

"Yes. Our house is that way." She pointed to the door to the right of where the four Xaxor stood.

The Xaxor were looking at the door to the left, waiting for us. The one holding the calculator hummed to the others, and they all turned and faced the other door.

"You knew it changed before they did! How did you know that?"

Our Xaxor was staring at Becky too. It couldn't understand English, but it had seen her point and seen its fellows turn.

Becky looked at all of us and shrugged. "It popped dut-dut. Next to the right door." She rubbed her right ear. "It was doing that last time, but I didn't know why."

I didn't like the way our Xaxor was looking at her.

"Stay away from Becky! You have the calculator. What more do you need?"

Our Xaxor lowered its eyes then scurried toward the rest of them. The other four sets of bug eyes stared at Becky hungrily.

Becky glared back.

"You can't be alone with them," I said.

"They're not going to get me." She raised both arms and wiggled her fingers, then turned her back and wiggled her butt at them.

My heart skipped a beat. "That's not funny, Becky. It's not funny. You can't provoke them."

She turned around again, arms folded. "Okay. Let's just go home."

"Okay." Without another word, I led her toward the waiting Xaxor, pushed my way in front of them, and went through the door.

27

THE HOUSE SEEMED TO BE EMPTY.

"Mom? Ip? Anyone?" I called.

No one answered, but it was clear someone had been here since we'd left. There were mud splotches on the carpet, marks I was sure we hadn't made after our foray into town. Also, the furniture in the living room had been haphazardly rearranged.

All five Xaxor followed us, touching things with their legs, poking their eyes into corners, humming to each other. Our Xaxor sat under the kitchen table, poking the bottom of it with three legs, lifting it slightly into the air.

"What's so great about a table?" asked Becky.

"I don't know, but someone else has been here, and it

wasn't Mom." I pointed to the mud stains. "I don't want to be here when they get back."

Something knocked on the kitchen window.

Becky and I froze. For the first time, I noticed that the curtains were not completely closed. They were open a few inches on the right side. Mom would never have done that. We always kept all the curtains tightly closed, all the time. I leaned over the sink, trying to see what was out there. There was only a little light from a far-away streetlight—

"Ah!" I jumped back.

Becky leaned over the sink, poking her head up. "Ip!"

I stepped forward again. Indeed, I could now see the outline of something blobby and two large, hard eyes. I struggled with the latch and pulled the window open. "Ip, is that you?" I whispered. I didn't know if our neighbors would be able to hear us, but I didn't want to take any chances.

"Ryan!" Ip whispered back. "You're safe!" Ip's face left the window, and after a loud thump, the kitchen door opened, revealing Ip, who squeezed his way through the door and into the kitchen, slamming the door behind him with a smash of his horn. It was immediately apparent where the mud had come from. He was covered in it almost completely from the middle down.

"Ip!" Becky ran forward and, unconcerned about the mud, gave him a big hug.

"My eyes, Becky! When was the last time you had a wash?"

"When has Becky washed? Look at this mud! Mom is going to kill us." But I ran over and gave Ip a hug, too. It was good to see someone I knew I could trust.

Gript popped up out of my backpack. "Were you going to let me out? I scratched my claws on that eye-rotting 'zipper'!"

"Infinitely sorry, Gript," I said. "Gript, meet Ip. Ip, Gript."

"A Brocine!" Ip exclaimed. "I never thought I'd see another one. Don't you folks live in packs?"

"Indeed," said Gript. "I've been specially trained to travel." He puffed up proudly, then deflated again.

"Another one?" I asked. "Do you mean you've seen Gript's family?"

"The ones in the zoo? They are your family?" Ip let out a wheezy sigh. "Yes, I've seen them."

"Are they all right?" Gript climbed up on my shoulder, claws digging into my neck. He scratched the welt from whatever the Xaxor had poked me with, and I squirmed.

"Seeing you now, I'm sure they aren't," said Ip. "They were lying together, looking not much aware of their surroundings."

"You said 'they,'" said Gript. "How many were there?"

Ip thought for a few seconds. One eye rolled toward the Xaxor who was still under the table. Without me noticing, the rest of the Xaxor had slipped silently over to us. "Xaxor," Ip observed. He looked back at us without further comment. "There were four of them. All rolled up together. Two your size and two smaller."

Gript squeaked and sat down on my shoulder. "All of them."

"And they're still in the zoo?" I asked.

Ip nodded. "They're in their sector."

I wasn't sure I wanted to ask the next question, but I didn't have to, because Ip guessed.

"Oscar is still alive. I saw Helena briefly, and it seemed all right."

I translated for Becky.

"But what happened to Ip?" she asked.

"Becky wants to know what happened to you. And so do I," I said. "What were you doing outside on Earth? What if someone saw you?"

"It was nighttime. Earth people are diurnal, right?"

I rolled my eyes. "Yes, but they still come out at night sometimes! Can't you see the streetlights?"

Ip shook his horn. "Well, no one saw me." Then his eyes brightened. "What a wonderful sky! The stars are so different from Hdkowl. And the air! I fear the Masters haven't taken such good care of our planet as they have of yours. I feel ten revolutions younger!"

"That's great, but did you get in trouble? Have the Masters asked about us? They know we're gone because Hon-tri-bum saw us on Brock. What did you tell them?" It all came out in a rush. I needed to know how much trouble we were in.

"Calm down, Ryan, you are safe here. I will tell you everything that happened." Ip eyed one of the kitchen chairs and wrenched it away from the table with a blobby arm.

Our Xaxor skittered out from under the table, joining its fellows, who stood in a row, watching us.

Ip plopped down in the chair, his too-big body oozing over the sides. Mud splashed onto the linoleum.

Becky jumped up on Ip's leg, and I took another chair. I gave our Xaxor a pointed look and turned the chair so that when I sat, I'd be facing away from all of them.

Ip looked from me to the row of Xaxor. "Is there something you need to tell me?"

"Just tell us what happened," I said, folding my arms.

"All right. Well, I led the Masters away and came back here as fast as I could. Got a message to the Hottini. Then I went back to the kitchen to get more Earth nutrition. You know, to make it seem like you were here. They just happened to have some insects. Anyway, I got you some if you're hungry."

I was hungry. I had barely eaten anything since the Brocine food the night before, but I shook my head.

"The first day, nobody noticed. I guess they were going to let you rest. But this morning, I was sitting in there watching the TV—some fascinating programs here on Earth—when I felt the message wind. I couldn't quite understand it—they calibrate it to your From chemistry, you know—but I knew they were calling you. I must admit I panicked a little. I went around opening and closing doors and things, jumping in and out of rooms, trying to make them think there were three people in here instead of just one Hdkowl-lll-ll-wyyyn. I don't know if it worked, but it certainly confused them. The wind became very strange, blowing around all over the place." Ip coughed. "If you find anything broken, that's why.

"Anyway, a couple of the Masters finally came looking for you. Yel-to-tor was one of them. It sounded like it knew you, calling out your name."

"It's my tutor," I said.

"Well, that explains it. Though my tutor never seemed to like me much. Anyway, I didn't know what to do, so I just hid outside."

"Outside! Was it daytime?"

"Yes, yes, but no one saw me. I was behind one of those things." Ip gestured to one of Mom's hanging plants.

My mouth dropped open.

"Don't look that way. It was bigger than that one. Anyway, the sun was too bright for anyone to see anything." Ip's giant, darkness-adapted eyes didn't blink.

"What's wrong?" asked Becky.

I gave a brief translation of what Ip had said so far.

She giggled. "I wonder if that kid saw him. You know, the one who stopped us when we went out."

"I wonder." It was too late now. If the Earth police were going to come, they would have come already. "What happened next?"

"Well, I crept right up to the window —" Ip pointed to the living room window, the one that, if the curtains were open, would have looked right out onto the front yard.

I groaned.

"To see if I could hear the Masters talking. We Hdkowl-lll-ll-wyyyns have exceptionally good hearing, you know." Ip shook his horn and smiled. I couldn't see anything that looked like ears anywhere on his body. "One says to the other, 'Bless my eyes! what happened here?' and the other one says, 'I don't know, but those froms are gone — and what happened to that Hdkowl-lll-ll-wyyyn?' That's when they all rushed in! A whole bunch of the Masters. I couldn't see much through the curtains except shadows, but they were all over. There was so much talking at first that I couldn't understand any of it, but then someone mentioned the Hottini and the

Brocine and some kind of emergency. It sounded like the planets had all moved around, but I must have heard that wrong."

"Did they say what happened to the planets?" Gript cut in.

"I don't know—it was all confused. Something about repairing a rift of variable infinity, whatever that means. Anyway, they kept saying 'stolen' and 'specimens,' and I realized they meant you children. I finally figured out that they were saying the Hottini had stolen you. Then someone said, really loud, 'Did they steal that Hd-kowl-lll-ll-wyyyn too?' Well, I figured the best thing to do would be to play along, so I ran through the door and fell down on my face right there." Ip pointed to the lino-leum in front of the front door. "I pretended to be out of my mind." He smiled.

"What did you tell them?" I asked, not sure I wanted to hear it.

"Well, they were trying to wake me up, asking me all these questions about what happened. I took a while to come around, played it up a little. Then I told them that the Hottini jumped out of nowhere, right there"—he pointed to the living room—"and they jumped on top of me, holding me down with their twisted claws—"

"Twisted claws? Ip, have you ever seen a Hottini's foot?"

Ip pulled his blobby arms closer to his body. "No."

"They don't have claws! They have fingers like ours." I wiggled them. "Eight on each foot."

"Well, no one questioned it!" Ip snapped. "I said that the Hottini pulled you two back through thin air, and I was so distraught and mad with grief that I hid in the foliage until the Masters showed up."

I sighed. It was better than nothing. At least the Pipe Men might still think none of this was our fault. "Okay, fine. Our story is that these Xaxor rescued us from the Hottini. We have no idea how anyone figured out how to open a portal. We've just been along for the ride the whole time."

Ip eyed the row of silent Xaxor. "What really happened?"

I gave him a brief synopsis, leaving the details out.

Ip shook with laughter. "Two days go by, and you've got everyone in the universe after you!"

Grip wriggled on my shoulder. "When did you see my family?"

"That was earlier today," said Ip. "I just came back here for the night in case something came up. And the

Earth air!" He breathed deeply, then exhaled with a sigh that nearly blew Gript off my shoulder.

"We can't keep wasting time!" said Gript. "It will be light on O-thul-ba before too long, right?"

I nodded. "It's close to Earth time."

"Then we must get to them! My children are not as well trained to be away from the pack as I am. They were only to be gone for a few days! From what you describe, they won't survive much longer!"

"He needs to rescue his family, and we need to get to Dad. I don't think we can wait until morning," I said to Becky.

Becky nodded. "You go help Gript. I can get to Dad. I think I figured the doors out."

"You think? That's a nice offer," I said, "but I'm not letting you out of my sight."

"I can do it!" She folded her arms. "They go duh-dum, duh-dum. Then dut-dut-dut. Then dut-dut. Dut-dut, and there's the right door."

"Maybe if we hurry to the hospital—"

"His family is going to die," Becky said. "I know how to get there." She glared at all the Xaxor. "I don't need them."

I didn't like the thought of her going alone, but the

hospital was close, and she had already proved that she could navigate the portals. And that she could act adorable enough to get in to see him. I couldn't let any of the Xaxor be alone with her. And if I went with her, and they stopped us from leaving, Gript might never find his family, and we might lose our chance to escape. *Listen to your sister, Ryan. She has a natural talent.* The memory of Front's voice vibrated inside my head. "Okay, and what are you going to say when the Pipe Men ask where I am?"

"You're at home sleeping, and I snuck out because I had to see my daddy." Becky scrunched up her face and gave her best puppy-dog eyes.

"Right, and how did we get home?"

Becky glared at the row of Xaxor again. "They rescued us while we were escaping from the Hottini and took us to Earth. We don't know how they know where Earth is."

"Right." I turned to Ip. "We can get to the Brocine sector through ours, right?"

Ip nodded.

"Can you take us there?"

Ip rolled his eyes toward the anxious Brocine on my shoulder, then toward the silent Xaxor. "All of you?"

I didn't know what to say. I had thought we needed the Xaxor, but now they seemed ominous, waiting to jump out and carry us away again. Did they really want to help us? Still, if we needed to make a quick escape, I was toast without the calculator. "Yes," I said. "All of us."

Ip looked from Becky and me to the Xaxor, then back again. He leaned in very close to me and whispered, "You know you can't trust a Xaxor, don't you, Ryan?" At least, he attempted to whisper. I was pretty sure that it came out loud enough for the Xaxor to hear.

"I know." I said it in my normal voice.

Ip leaned back. "All right, then! To the Brocine sector before the sun comes up!"

28

"**HOW AM I GOING TO FIND YOU AGAIN?**" Becky asked. I couldn't see her face in the darkness of the closet. She sounded a little teary.

"Once Dad is okay, you try to meet us at the Brocine sector in the zoo. If you can't get there, you take Mom and Dad to Front. Do you think you can find Frontringhor?"

"Yes. But what if Mom and Dad don't believe me?"

"You have to make them believe you. You got the antidote, didn't you? Mom sent you all the way across the universe for it." I couldn't help but start getting angry. Mom had sent us on this crazy quest without having any idea what she was getting us into. "If she's going to make us go through all this, she has to believe us and do what we say!"

Becky was quiet for a second. "I'm scared," she whispered.

I was scared too. "There's nothing to be scared of," I said. "The Pipe Men don't want to hurt us."

"Then why are we trying to escape? I don't want to live on some other planet! Froms don't know anything. I want to learn about þok from the Pipe Men and meet lots of new Froms and go through the portals."

I wasn't sure I wanted to escape either, not unless we had to. I would miss Yel-to-tor, and even Hon-tri-þum and the other spectators. "Well, then there's nothing to be afraid of. If they catch you, they'll just keep you here." And keep us from ever going back to Earth. I tried to push the picture of the Earth sky out of my mind, but it kept pressing behind my eyes. I felt like I was missing something, not being there.

She was quiet.

I didn't know what to say.

"I'm afraid they'll take me someplace different from you," she said.

"I'm not going to let that happen." I pulled her into a hug. I couldn't remember the last time I'd really hugged her.

"Okay," she said. "Bye."

"Bye." There was an almost imperceptible buzz as she stepped into the portal. I stepped out of Mom and Dad's closet, wiping tears away from my eyes. I didn't want anyone to see them, but everyone was standing in the bedroom, waiting.

"Come on," I said, brushing past all of them. I didn't wait to see who was behind me, but I could hear them following. Ip lumbered and clumped, and I could even hear the Xaxor, treading lightly but humming a little—and stinking. Their smell probably hadn't really gotten worse, but I felt like I was right under their bellies again.

Gript rustled in my backpack.

"Quit moving," I snapped.

He rustled for another second, then was silent.

I stepped into the living room closet, then straight through the portal into our sector without stopping. Though it was dark, tiny lights dotted the tops of the invisible walls, just enough for me to make out the basics. There was the table where Becky and I had sat just a couple of days ago, eating our lunch in front of the Pipe Men. There was the spot where I'd talked to Hon-tri-bum and its little five-eyed friend. I'd had no idea that Hon-tri-bum was such an important person. No idea that the Pipe Men were feared for their immense power over something I didn't understand. No idea that they kidnapped children and exploited planets, or that we were really and truly captives.

There was the table where Yel-to-tor had taught me their language and tried to teach me math. Just enough so that I could repeat it, but never enough so that I could really understand, assuming I was too stupid to figure it out. Beyond that was the perfectly calibrated play structure for Earth children and the table where Becky used to sit with her tutor, Bre-zon-air, understanding more than I did, proving them wrong.

She should be entering the hospital by now. What would she find? The Pipe Men we thought we knew, who would take her to our parents, or the Pipe Men everyone else in the universe saw? I had never seen our zoo sector this dark and deserted before. It looked like a completely different place.

Ip globbed past me and waved for me to follow.

As I started walking, letting my boots spring off the familiar rubber ground, our Xaxor slunk up alongside me. It held out the tablet, the words barely visible in the dim light.

They found us. I didn't bring you to them.

I pushed the tablet back. "You poisoned us." I poked angrily at the welt on my neck.

We could not get away. It seemed easier on you. It stared up at me with two eyes, keeping one on our path. We were passing the play structure, heading for the edge of our sector, toward a part of the zoo I'd never seen.

"You told them about the calculator."

The Xaxor typed furiously. I did not tell them. You think we're stupid because we look like tiny creatures on your planet with no brains. You and the Hottini created a rift of variable infinity. Everyone was chasing you. And we disappeared from the Hottini ship, only to be found on Brock. Do you think the Xaxor slept through all of it?

I hadn't thought about that. It seemed obvious, now that it had said it. That I couldn't hide what I had while at the same time jumping all over the universe. Front must have realized that. But why did he give it to me? Maybe it was Front's fault that I was in this mess. We could have found the door. The Hottini would have taken us to the Brocine. The Brocine would have helped us. Everything would have been fine if Front hadn't given me something everyone was willing to chase me around the universe for. I wasn't ready to let the Xaxor off the hook, though. It had poisoned us instead of waking us up and warning us.

The Xaxor kept typing. You have started this war. We only want to end up with something when it is over.

I had started a war? No one had shot each other, the way they did on Earth TV. But what if that changed? What if people got hurt, all because I went running across the universe without knowing what I was doing?

Ip turned his horn and touched something invisible with it, then went on walking through the invisible door. The sector just beyond ours didn't look much different, but I had never been there before. I had seen the Froms who lived there only from a distance. Thin, jagged creatures that crawled on the ground, they had never approached us, and we had never approached them. I didn't know whether they lived on their own planet like we did or whether they were forced to stay in their sector twenty-four and a half hours a day.

The ground didn't change as I walked through, and neither did the air. Surely something so different from us would need to live differently? There were large holes in the ground marked by mounds of Pipe Man fabric, and the area reminded me of our so-called play structure, so different from the real thing. How would these creatures live if they had the choice? How would I?

It took at least fifteen minutes to walk through the sector. Our Xaxor tripped quietly next to me, and the others stayed a little ways behind. It gave me a lot of time to think. About what my life would be like if I could go outside on Earth more often, if I could go to school and have Earth friends. If I could have friends at all who weren't aliens constantly commenting on my body parts. Outside of Becky, regular visitors like Hon-tri-þuʍ were my best friends. And I was just an exhibit to them. No better than a pet. But what if I was like all the other Earth people? They didn't even know about the Pipe Men or any of the Froʍs. They didn't know about portals, or space travel, or þok. What would it be like to never see another face from a different planet, to be ignorant like a goldfish swimming around and around in a tiny bowl?

Ip took us through another invisible wall, then another. The landscape changed from bumpy little hills and caves to tall trees, then to thick bushes. We came to a sector that had both giant caves and tall trees, rising far above our heads on our left, where I imagined there must be a portal be that led to a giant, monster planet.

One thing was always the same — the ground was always made of Pipe Man fabric, the same color and texture everywhere.

No one seemed to be awake. I had never wondered about the zoo at night, never tried to come back and see what it looked like. We were told to go, and we went. We were told to come back, and we came back.

Ip led us through another door, another invisible barrier that I had never thought about trying to walk through. The landscape was flat, peppered with basketball-sized holes, spaced at regular intervals a few yards apart.

Ip held out a blobby arm. "The Brocine are here somewhere," he whispered. "I don't know where they sleep."

I looked around to make sure that no Pipe Men had come out, set my backpack on the ground, and unzipped it. "Gript," I whispered, "Ip says this is it."

Gript crawled out of the backpack on all fours and stood on the Pipe Man fabric ground, claws bouncing against the rubber. He looked up at me. "It's dry." He walked over to one of the holes and peered down it.

I leaned over him, but it was too dark for me to see.

Gript squeaked something in their language into the

hole, then waited for a response, but there was nothing. "I need to go down."

"Okay." I pulled a roll of twine out of the backpack and tied the end around Gript's waist.

Gript tugged on it to make sure it was secure, then jumped into the hole. The twine tightened slowly in my hands.

I looked around at the barren landscape, the silent Xaxor, Ip standing too still. The lights were as dim as before, but they began to stand out, to make me more nervous now that we weren't moving. The Pipe Men didn't even need this much light to see. They could be watching us right now, with no trouble at all.

"Ryan."

"Who said that?" I whispered. It wasn't Ip, and it couldn't have been the Xaxor.

Ip looked around him.

"You let me see him! That's my daddy! I want to see my daddy!"

"Becky?" It was her voice, but I couldn't tell where it was coming from.

"I . . . WANT . . . TO SEE . . . MY . . . DADDY!" Becky screamed. She was jumping up and down now.

I couldn't see it, but I knew it. I'd seen her act this way a thousand times. I just never thought I'd be happy to hear it. So much for acting adorable.

"Honey, hush. Stop—" Mom's voice.

"DAD-DY!"

"Becky?" It was too quiet. Whatever was going on, I was still tuned in to it, but I didn't hear any more voices.

Our Xaxor was suddenly next to me, waving two legs, pulling out its tablet with a third.

The twine jerked, unrolling so quickly that the friction of the twine ball burned my hands, and I dropped it. The Xaxor caught it with one leg, and I quickly grabbed it again.

"Gript? Are you all right?" I called.

"Put them together," said a strange voice in my head. A Pipe Man.

"Honey, stop. Calm down. You're going to hurt yourself. You could unbind its arms. It's going to hurt itself."

Becky needs your help, the Xaxor typed.

"You can hear it too?" I didn't wait for an answer. "I need you to hold Gript."

The Xaxor took the ball of twine and wrapped one leg around it several times. With two other legs, it hummed something to its fellows. The one with the calculator came forward.

"I need to go back to our house," I said. The portal in Mom and Dad's closet was the only place I could start from to find the hospital. The four Xaxor hummed to each other, examining the calculator. Then one pressed a button, and a portal opened. "Thank you," I said, jumping into it. As I was going, I realized that I wasn't sure I could find the hospital, much less get back to the Brocine sector. But I couldn't stop to let myself worry. I had to find Becky before something worse happened.

29

NOTHING WAS RECOGNIZABLE. The doors weren't all the same shape, weren't even any shape. They swirled and changed and blended into each other, changing colors, from pure black to speckled with red, blue, green. The walls and floors melted into each other and pulsed, red globs moving and bubbling like baking dough. The floor shifted under me, and I fell, catching myself with my hands. The floor was warm, lifelike. I had no idea where in the passage I was.

"Go forward, Ryan."

I crawled forward. The floor smoothed a little, as if it was trying to make way for me, but it kept bubbling. My hands and knees sank in, and it took a lot of effort to move.

"Front?" I asked, struggling to breathe with the

effort and with the heaviness of the air. I didn't know how he could be here, but it was his voice.

"I could not tell you before. I am sorry."

"What couldn't you tell me? Where are you?" I was passing doors, but I wasn't sure how many, the way they were all swirled up together. I couldn't guess how far I'd gone.

"You have helped me a great deal. I am close to being free."

"Front, please. I don't understand what's going on!"

"I will explain it to you, but you must get to your family. I'm afraid I've made a mess of things."

"What do you mean?"

"In gaining my freedom, I have caused discord among the species of your known universe, and I have hurt you. I am sorry."

I didn't have time to think about all this. "How do I get to the hospital?"

"It will be three doors from here, on your left."

I got there. The wall seemed to be one long door of many swirling colors, but short, barely tall enough for me to crawl through. "Is this all one door?"

"Just go forward."

I did as I was told, and I found myself staring at

the mouth and bottom two eyes of a Pipe Man. Out of my peripheral vision, I saw at least two more. I didn't have time to think. I just jumped forward and butted the first one with my head. It fell backward, landed with a thump, and rolled a little. I scrambled over it and got to my feet. The other two were coming toward me. I kicked one in the mouth and then the other. They fell on top of each other like Pick-up Sticks.

I looked around, trying to get my bearings. I was in the hospital, the part where there were long, skinny beds for Pipe Men. There was a Pipe Man in one of the beds, but no one else. This room had been completely empty before, and there hadn't been a portal here. I realized there wasn't a portal here now either. Wherever I had come from, it was gone.

The Pipe Man in the bed was covered in assistant wires. It was sitting up a little, though, bending at one crinkly spot in the middle, staring at me with ten blue eyes.

"I'm sorry—I had to!" I said to it.

The Pipe Men on the floor were rolling, and I heard buzzing. Wires were coming down, lowering methodically from their usual perches just beneath the ceiling. They came slowly toward the fallen Pipe Men, pulling extra wire from somewhere unseen to make a U shape that stretched as it dropped toward the Masters.

I slid through the narrow passage between the beds and ran to the hallway and through the door, to where the Froms were supposed to be. The buzzing of the wires got louder behind me.

"Mom! Becky!" I glanced behind me and saw that the U-shaped wires were underneath the Pipe Men that I'd knocked down, slowly lifting them right end up.

"Ryan?" It was my mom, calling from somewhere not far off, from behind one of the curtains.

Three more Pipe Men came out from one of the curtain-enclosed rooms and whooshed toward me. I thought fast. The other Pipe Men had gone down with barely any effort on my part. They were so fragile, they needed their assistants to do everything for them. I could at least knock these three down for long enough to free Becky and get the antidote from her. I kicked.

The Pipe Man in the middle fell on its back, letting out a high-pitched screech. The other two jumped at me, propelling themselves with sudden blasts of air. I punched one in the eye and then the other, and they fell. This was too easy. I turned to keep running and ran my stomach right into an assistant wire. It pushed me back toward the fallen Pipe Men, as if it were straining to reach them. I dropped to the ground and slid under it.

The Pipe Men rolled around, trying to get into the cradles the wires made. Fortunately, the wires didn't seem to care about me, but were only interested in righting the Pipe Men.

I made it to the curtain and pulled it open. There was Dad, lying in the bed, looking the same as he'd looked two days ago, covered in wires and not moving. Mom sat on the floor, hands tangled in wires. Becky sat next to Mom, her hands also tangled in wires and her mouth wrapped in Pipe Man fabric.

"It's going to be okay," I said. "You still have the antidote?" I didn't wait for her to try to answer, but reached into her pocket and pulled it out.

"You had the antidote? Oh, baby." Mom struggled, trying to stand, but her legs were also tangled in assistant wires.

"I'll explain everything," I said. "Praise pupils, I hope this works." Gript had never told me where to inject the antidote. He couldn't know anything about human anatomy anyway. I was just going to have to guess. I took a deep breath and stuck the tiny syringe into Dad's neck, pushing the needle all the way in. When it was empty, I pulled it out again. A few drops of blood dripped from the wound. I pressed the sleeve of my tunic against it. "Come on, Dad," I whispered.

Something thumped behind me. It was Becky, hopping on her butt.

"Okay, I'm coming." I let go of Dad, and the bleeding seemed to have stopped. Then I unwrapped the Pipe Man fabric from Becky's head.

"Behind you!" she yelled.

I kicked a Pipe Man coming through the curtain.

It fell backward into an assistant wire and, in seconds, was upright again.

"You must stop," it said.

"What are you going to do?" I yelled. "You can't do anything without your wires. You can't stop me!"

Suddenly, all the wires pulled away from Dad at once. I ducked, but some hit me, stinging like whips, knocking me on top of Becky. More wires also wrapped around Mom's belly.

"Ow!" Becky rolled out from under me, but wires slid over my head and wrapped around her.

The Pipe Man was coming closer, leaning over me. Its top-hole dripped drool.

"What are you going to do, spit on me?" I yelled.

A glob of spit landed on my forehead. It burned a little.

The Pipe Man scrunched up its top eyes, laughing.

Some of the air whooshed out of the room. I leaned my head back and saw it—a portal, giant, swirling, and deep black with just a touch of red. It was right behind Dad's bed.

"You see that?" I said. "I can open a portal whenever I want to. I know more than you do." At least, Front apparently could. I hoped it was him.

With a whoosh of air, Dad's bed began to roll. It was being sucked straight into the swirling portal.

"Come on! We have to go after it." I struggled to get the wires off me, but they pushed back and cut into my skin.

"Ah!" Becky screeched as she was lifted off the ground by the wires. She hung there in midair, nine eyes up. Mom was next. She chirped more than screamed, staring wide-eyed at Dad's disappearing bed.

"It's okay, Mom, he's going to be fine, he—aah!" I couldn't help but scream myself, being lifted suddenly into the air, even though I'd known it was coming. I squirmed against the wires. They cut into me more, but I didn't care. "You see that?! I'll open one right in front of you and you'll never get back!"

There were four Pipe Men now, all with wires behind them, ready to catch them if they fell again. One of them was carrying a calculator in its top-hole. It floated underneath me to the edge of the portal, where the remainder of Dad's bed was disappearing into the breach. Lights were flashing all over its calculator, like I'd never seen on mine. Another Pipe Man floated next to the first, tapped the calculator with a stylus, and blinked eyes at the other.

"You won't be able to close it!"

"Let me down, you overgrown drainpipes!" yelled Becky.

"Don't struggle, honey. You're going to hurt yourself," said Mom.

Another portal opened right above the two Pipe Men. They both turned up their top three eyes, and the portal began slowly sucking them upward. The calculator clattered to the ground, followed by the stylus. As the stylus hit, a portal opened right below the calculator. It began sucking the Pipe Men back toward it. The other two Pipe Men sped forward. One tipped its top-hole over into the bottom portal, so that two, then three, then four of its eyes disappeared into it.

The fourth Pipe Man maneuvered itself right under me and looked up. "Close it."

"Let us down first."

"Eeep!" The Pipe Man who had stuck its top into the lower portal screeched as it was suddenly sucked all the way in. The other two were hanging in the air, halfway into the upper portal and halfway out. Their bottoms flailed around, a mouth and four eyes each.

"If you don't close this portal, you will never return to Earth!" one shouted. I had never heard a Pipe Man yell before today, or really express any major emotion. Then again, I'd never seen one dangling unceremoniously from an interspace portal.

"You can't get out," Becky taunted. "You . . . don't . . . know . . . how . . . to . . . fix . . . it."

Why did she have to suddenly figure out how to make a complete sentence in their language? She was just going to make things worse.

"But I can get out!" She wriggled through two of the

wires holding her and jumped on top of the Pipe Man who was still standing. The Pipe Man bent its body and thrashed, but she jumped off it, stood up straight, and gave it a good kick. Her hands were still tied behind her back. She looked up at Mom and me. "Just wriggle side to side. They're not made for holding Froms."

I started wriggling around.

"No, not like that, like this." She twisted back and forth quickly from side to side, then turned and gave the Pipe Man on the ground another kick. It wriggled backward.

I tried it the way she showed me, and after a few wriggles, I found myself starting to fall through the wires. Before I could think about how I was going to catch myself, I was on the ground, flat on my face.

"Are you okay?" Becky leaned over me as I lifted myself up. My nose hurt, but I didn't think it was broken.

"I'm fine—Mom, are you trying it?" I unraveled the wires from Becky's hands while Mom wriggled back and forth. "Try not to fall headfirst." I reached out to catch her and she fell into me, almost knocking me over. I quickly unwrapped her hands and legs. "Let's go!"

"But where are we going? What's in there?" Mom asked.

"I don't know, but it's our friend opening the portals. Besides, we have to get Dad!"

More wires were dropping, heading for the Pipe Man on the floor. We had to dodge them to make it to the portals.

"I don't think we want to go in that one," I said, pointing to the one on the floor, where the Pipe Man had disappeared. "Dad went that way. So we have to jump. Mom?"

With a little spring, Mom jumped over the portal on the ground and disappeared into the place the wall should be.

"Becky?"

She jumped.

"You can let them go," I said, hoping Front would hear me. "Just close the portal after me."

The portal on the ground sucked itself closed. The two Pipe Men who were hanging in the air fell abruptly onto the now-solid floor. They both let out squeaky metallic groans and wriggled to straighten their bodies. A third Pipe Man dropped heavily out of the portal onto its fellows and lay flat, eyes up. I recognized it as the one that had been sucked into the other portal. All nine of its dazed eyes blinked at me. After this, I was pretty sure we weren't going to be able to go home.

"I'm infinitely sorry," I said. "I really am," and I jumped over the Pipe Men and into the wall.

3 0

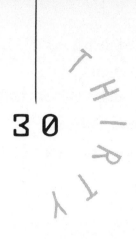

I STOPPED AFTER A STEP through the portal, still feeling the buzzing, tiny pinpricks poking at me from all sides. I was back in the Brocine zoo sector, on Pipe Man fabric ground, looking up at the dark O-thʋl-ban sky. I blinked and shook to get the pinpricks off me, but they lingered. It took me a few seconds to see straight.

Dad's bed was in front of me. He was still lying on it. Mom was on one side, and Becky was on the other. Ip was next to Becky, wrapping her in one large blobby arm. There were Xaxor standing at the head of the bed, four of them.

I blinked again, not sure I was seeing right. But I was. And Dad was waking up, looking around, even more confused than I was. He looked at Becky and Ip, at Mom, and at me.

"Where am I?" He took a deep breath and lifted himself up onto his elbows.

"We're in the zoo, honey," said Mom, "in the Brocine sector."

"Why am I in bed? And why is it dark?"

"There was an accident. One of the Brocine children stabbed you with its nose. You couldn't wake up." Mom tried to hold back tears, but sniffed.

"I remember," said Dad. "It wouldn't eat. I prodded it with the dish. It squeaked and jumped on me. That's it—then I was here. What happened?"

"We got an antidote, Dad," I broke in. "You're going to be fine, but I don't have time to explain everything. We have to get out of here before the Pipe Men get their act together and stop us from going."

"Going? Where are we going?" He sat up all the way and swung his legs over the side of the bed, toward Mom.

"Take it easy, honey," said Mom.

"We don't have time for him to take it easy," I said. "Can you walk?"

"I think so. Just give me a second. I'll be fine." He

shook his head as if to clear it and then froze, seeing the Xaxor for the first time.

"They're Xaxor, Dad. They're here to help us escape."

"Escape?" Dad didn't take his eyes off the Xaxor. "What are we escaping from?"

"From the zoo, from the Pipe Men! And we have to go. They're going to be coming after us."

"Hold on a second, son. Where are we supposed to be escaping to? This is our home."

"Not anymore, Dad. We had to go to Brock to get the antidote and—just trust me!" I looked around, trying to take stock of where everyone was.

"To Brock? You mean, the Brocine home planet?"

Our Xaxor was behind me, its eyes turned away from us.

"Mom, Becky, help Dad up. And you"—I pointed to the four Xaxor—"get ready to open a portal. We have to go anywhere, now!"

"We don't need them," said Becky. "We have Front to help us."

"Front?" I called.

"Ryan." Front's voice in my head was faint, as if coming from a great distance.

We need to get out of here, I thought.

"They're inside me. All around me."

What? Front, what's wrong?

Front made a tiny sound, like a groan or a sigh, and then he was silent.

"Inside him!" Becky said. "How?"

I shook my head. We'd have to help him, but first we had to get out of the zoo. I pointed at the four Xaxor again. "Just get the calculator ready!" I ran to our Xaxor and saw what it was looking at. Gript was huddled with four other Brocine, two the size of Gript and two much smaller. "You got them! How are they?"

Gript looked up at me, tears in his eyes. "Not well at all." He squeaked something in their language. One of the adult Brocine was sitting, but the other three were lying on the ground, looking asleep, passed out, or worse. They stank as bad as a whole cave full.

"Are they alive?" I bent down to get a closer look.

Gript held out a paw. "Careful, Earth. The children can't control themselves."

I pulled back a little, to what I hoped was out of jumping range, though from the look of it, none of them was in any shape to jump. "What's wrong with them? Can we move them?"

"We will have to—they need water—and other Brocine. No Brocine should go so long without its pack." Gript bared his teeth, pushed out his nose, and flexed the claws on all four paws.

"I can take two in my backpack." I pointed to it. "And Becky can take two. Will they be okay? Becky, come over here!"

We took what water we had and tried to make Gript's family drink a little, but the little ones were barely able to sip. In the background, Mom was trying to explain to Dad what had gone on. She didn't quite tell it right, but at least she understood that we had to get out of here. Dad was arguing, saying the Pipe Men had been good to us.

"They wouldn't let me take you to a doctor!" Mom whisper-yelled. "They were just going to let you die."

"You were going to take me to Earth? What if something happened?"

"What could happen? You were going to die!"

"So you sent the kids to the Hottini? How did you think that would work out?"

"Like it did, Oscar. They found you a cure."

"And now we're running away? To where? Earth?"

Dad almost shouted. "You want to live with Earth people?"

"We are Earth people," said Mom, much more quietly.

"We're not Earth people anymore," said Dad. "We're educated. We live among the Masters."

"They teach us that they're special," said Becky. "But they're not. You just have to kick them, and they fall over."

"Earth isn't safe anyway," said Mom. "There are Masters there. We have to find somewhere else to go."

Dad stared at her, shaking his head.

Our Xaxor dipped one of its legs in my water bottle and gently pushed it into one of the Brocine children's mouths. It repeated the trick with another leg and the other child. One of the children began to stir. The Xaxor kept doing this until a good amount of water had gotten into both of them, then tried it with the adults. After a few more minutes of this, and Mom and Dad arguing about whether we should run away and where to, the Brocine were all awake, although not moving much.

Grip and his adult children managed to have a brief

discussion in their language before one of them started coughing. The Xaxor fed her the rest of the water.

The lights came on. The whole sector was lit up as brightly as the dim O-thul-ban daytime.

"Come on, get in! Becky, help us!"

Becky opened her backpack and reached out for one of the children.

"No! Wait!" I held my hand up.

The Xaxor understood and wrapped a leg around the child, gently moving it into Becky's backpack, keeping its nose away from her. One of the adults was able to crawl in on his own. The Xaxor lifted the other baby, and Gript helped the other adult into my backpack. They squeaked something at each other, and I zipped it almost all the way. Gript jumped onto my shoulder.

Pipe Men were all around the outside of the sector, lining the invisible walls. They were many different heights, many different colors of eyes. All together, closing in, they looked alien in a way they never had before.

"Front?" I whispered.

There was no response. I didn't hear anything from that place in my mind where he had spoken. I looked at the row of Xaxor. Three of them were circled around the one with the calculator, hiding it from view, facing the Pipe Men. Becky, our Xaxor, and Gript and I moved slowly toward Dad's bed. Ip had curled into a ball next to it. With none of his face showing, the horn looked like some kind of desert plant growing out of a rock.

I raised my arms. "We are infinitely sorry for the disturbance," I said. "We didn't mean to hurt anyone." I cocked my head toward the group of Xaxor.

They hummed at each other furiously.

"The Hottini kidnapped us," I yelled. "These Xaxor rescued us!"

"I don't think that story's going to work," said Becky.

Dad stood up and raised his arms. He stumbled forward into the bed, but recovered and raised his arms again. "There is a misunderstanding, honored Masters. We are infinitely sorry to have caused offense. My children did not understand their actions."

"Front," I whispered, "come on, where are you?"

"Front, help us," said Becky.

A stream of Pipe Men began floating through an invisible door, coming toward us. I recognized the first one by its sixteen many-shaded purple eyes.

"Ry-an," said Hon-tri-bum. "Beck-y, Os-car, and

Hel-ena." It turned three eyes toward my parents and blinked, acknowledging them. "We will take you back to your sector. You will not be harmed."

I brought my arms down and bowed forward. "Master Hon-tri-bum, Minister," I said, "what will happen to these Froms who helped us escape from the terrible Hottini monsters?"

Pipe Men were beginning to circle the four Xaxor. Two held calculators in their top-holes, and three others held styluses.

"True to their race, they have stolen something of great value to us," said Hon-tri-bum.

"It was the Hottini that took us, honored Master. The Xaxor rescued us."

Hon-tri-bum studied me with most of its eyes, keeping only four on the others around us.

I held Becky's hand tighter. I didn't like the way Hon-tri-bum was looking at me. *Front*, I thought. Where was he? If he could open a portal just a few minutes ago anywhere he wanted, why couldn't he do that now? And why wasn't he talking?

All at once, Hon-tri-bum flashed all of its eyes toward the invisible door the Pipe Men had come through.

More Pipe Men appeared, floating out of the shadows beyond the lights.

At first I didn't see them because they were surrounded by tall Pipe Men, but as the group came closer, I saw two Hottini among the Pipe Men bodies. They held their heads up, but they were walking gingerly, almost shuffling along the artificial ground. The Pipe Men went two by two through the invisible door, pushing the Hottini into single file. As they came closer, I could see that they were not wearing any coverings. Their blue hair was dull and matted against their bodies, and they were barefoot.

Grav-e glared at me as they approached. Tast-e took in the scene, fixing his eyes on the group of Xaxor.

"These Froms have failed to adequately explain how they created the rift that nearly sucked Hottin into Brock," said Hon-tri-bum.

"What?" said Dad.

Gript dug his claws into my shoulder.

I looked at Grav-e, trying to get something from him that would give me a hint of what they'd said about us, but I couldn't read anything in those angry purple eyes. "They have some kind of lab," I said. "We had to go through it to escape. That's how they opened the portal." I tried to remember what Hon-tri-bum had called it. "The rift of variable infinity."

"We have examined the lab," said Hon-tri-bum. "It is not capable of creating such a rift alone." It shifted three more eyes toward the Xaxor.

Becky's hand was sweating, and so was mine. There were too many for us to kick over. No way to escape without the calculator or Front.

"There are none behind us," Gript whispered. His nose was dangerously close to my cheek as he leaned into my ear.

"The Xaxor have stolen something more valuable than you, Ry-an. My question is, where did they get it?"

"What is it talking about, Ryan?" Dad put his arm around both Becky and me. "My children haven't done anything wrong, honored Master. There has been some terrible mistake."

A great, awful humming came from the four Xaxor. One of the Pipe Men butted a Xaxor with its top-hole. That Xaxor kicked with all of its legs, and the other three jumped on the Pipe Man. More Pipe Men floated over to butt the ball of flailing Xaxor. Xaxor legs wrapped around Pipes, squeezing them. Several Pipe Men came streaming in from outside, holding penlike instruments in their tops, and poked the Xaxor with them. The Xaxor jumped off the Pipe Men and rolled into four tiny balls. As the last Xaxor balled up, the calculator appeared as if out of thin air and fell to the rubbery ground with a soft thump. Its Xaxor leg–like wrapping left no doubt where it had come from.

The two Pipe Men who had calculators whooshed over to it. They sank down, bending eye by eye until half of their bodies were bent horizontal over the ground, and held their calculators out. Pipe Men with regular styluses bent over them and began pressing parts of the screens and rubbing the jagged edges. The three calculators buzzed and then lights flashed, connecting the three calculators in a web of lights.

"Bless my eyes," said Mom.

Dad stared at me.

Points of light burst into being above the three calculators, one after the other. I recognized the pattern from the Hottini ship—a star map. Stars flashed by as the Pipe Men moved the display by tapping the side of it with one of their styluses. After several passes, the stars suddenly disappeared, replaced by blackness swirling with points of red, just like a portal in the passage.

Hon-tri-þum stared at it for several long seconds, blinked something at the others, then turned ten of its eyes toward me. "Frontringhor."

"Where is that?" Dad looked at the swirling black, then back at me. "Did you use that device to go to some other planet?"

"It was an accident," I said. I turned to Hon-tri-þum. "It was an accident. I got lost in the passage when I was trying to visit my parent in the hospital." I pointed to Dad. "I don't know where I went. I was just in a cave, and I knew it was the wrong door, so I came back out again." But how could I explain the calculator? I shouldn't have said I was in the passage. I should have acted like I didn't understand.

"How do you know what that is?" Hon-tri-þum flashed four eyes at the calculator and the swirling black. I didn't know which part he meant.

"I don't!"

"Raise your arms when you speak to the Masters," said Dad.

I raised my arms.

"How did you open the portal in the hospital?" asked Hon-tri-þum.

"I didn't!"

More Pipe Men were coming into the sector. Many were holding the penlike things that had shocked the Xaxor into little balls. They weren't helpless anymore. I couldn't just kick them and get away. But Hon-tri-þum didn't have a weapon, and so far, there still weren't any Pipe Men behind us.

Gript jumped off my shoulder and landed on Hon-tri-þum's top-hole.

The Pipe Man screeched and squiggled around as Gript dug his claws in.

"Come on!" I yelled. I grabbed Becky, turned, and ran toward the invisible door to the next enclosure, the one where everything was giant. I couldn't be sure, but I had to hope that those creatures didn't live only in the zoo, that there was a portal somewhere in their sector. And I had to hope that everyone would follow. I stole a glance behind me.

Hon-tri-þum was sliding along at a wild pace after us, still trying to shake Gript. Our Xaxor jumped on Hon-tri-þum's back and wrapped its legs around it.

Hon-tri-bum screeched louder and fell over right onto its eyes, Gript still on the back of its top-hole. The other Xaxor leapt out of their balls in a coordinated poof and jumped on the Pipe Men in front of them.

Ip rolled out of his ball and pushed Mom and Dad forward. Dad was arguing with Ip, but Ip kept pushing, and Mom pulled Dad along. The other Pipe Men were coming faster.

"Come on!" I yelled. "This way!" I kept running, through the door and into the next sector. Even with all the tall trees, there was no place to hide. They were spaced too far apart. My only choice was to head for the giant caves and hope there was a portal in one of them, and that I'd find it.

"Which one do you think has a portal?" I asked.

"That one." Becky pointed to the third cave down.

I ran. Noises were coming from behind us, voices in English and Pipe Man, Xaxor hums, and screeches that could have come from anyone. I wanted to keep everyone together, but my first priority was Becky. I had to get her out of here. I pulled her into the third cave.

"Stay back, or my friend pokes the Minister in the eyelid!" Ip's voice came from behind me.

"That's right," squeaked Gript. "If you like Hon-tri-bum, honored Master, Minister of Trade, and all that, you'll float right back!"

Mom and Dad appeared inside the cave. It was so dark that we could barely see anything, but the cave appeared to be empty except for damp rocks.

"They're holding Hon-tri-bum hostage?" I whispered.

"We can never come back," said Dad. He put his hands to his forehead and rubbed his eyes.

"There's a portal in here," said Mom, rubbing Dad's back. "It's popping. Duh-dum."

"Becky thinks there is too," I said.

"That's my girl," said Mom, smiling at Becky. "Go. We'll follow you."

"Not without Ip and Gript," said Becky. "We can't leave them."

"We can't leave the Xaxor either," I said.

"Yes, we can," said Becky.

"Don't come after us!" said Ip. "If you hurt any one of us—the Earth people, the Xaxor, the Brocine—"

"What about Grav-e and Tast-e?" asked Becky. "Where are they?"

"I don't know," I said. "We can't worry about them right now."

Becky pulled her hand out of mine, and before I could stop her, she had run back out of the cave. I followed, and so did Mom and Dad. There was Ip, who had Hon-tri-bum wrapped in a giant blobby arm. Gript was perched on top of the same arm, claws digging into Ip's hide, nose less than an inch from one of Hon-tri-bum's eyes.

"You have to let Grav-e and Tast-e come with us, too," Becky said.

Four Xaxor skittered past us and into the cave, but our Xaxor stopped when it reached us and stood next to me and Mom and Dad. I rushed forward and grabbed Becky's hand again. We were facing rows of Pipe Men, more Pipe Men than I'd ever seen together before.

"Translate," said Becky.

"We want our Hottini friends, Grav-e and Tast-e," I said. "Let them go or we'll . . . we'll . . . cut one of Hon-tri-bum's eyes out." I hoped I'd have a chance to make it up to Hon-tri-bum later—and that the Pipe Men wouldn't call my bluff.

Ip pointed one pomegranate eye toward me, then

shifted his vision back to face the crowd. "That's right," said Ip. "Those Hottini need to come too."

Some of the Pipe Men blinked at each other. Others spoke in whispers that I couldn't hear. All the eyes stared at us, ten plus twelve plus sixteen plus eight plus ten . . . I gripped Becky's hand harder.

A path opened up between the lines of Pipe Men, and slowly, Grav-e and Tast-e shuffled forward, their bare handlike feet scraping awkwardly against the springy artificial ground. The Pipe Men let them step past their perimeter, toward us. Grav-e looked at me, head held high, then turned his eyes to Becky. He nodded to us, ever so slightly. "Thank you," he said, and both Hottini continued past us into the cave.

"Come on," I said, "let's go." I waved to Ip.

Gript moved his nose a little farther from Hon-tri-bum's eye.

Ip pulled Hon-tri-bum slowly backward.

"Mom, Dad, come on." I pulled Becky, following Mom and Dad into the cave.

"We'll let it go as soon as we're safely away," said Ip. "We won't hurt it unless you try to stop us." He backed into the cave, still holding Hon-tri-bum around the eyes. "We got everyone, Ryan?"

I squinted through the dim light. We had Mom, Dad, and Becky; Grav-e and Tast-e; our Xaxor; Ip, Gript, and the other Brocine in our backpacks; and way back in the cave, huddled together, the other four Xaxor. "We have everyone."

"Okay, let's find a portal and get out of here," said Ip.

I led the way to the back of the cave. It was even bigger than it had seemed at first. As Becky and I reached the four Xaxor, they circled around us. For the first time, their presence was actually comforting.

"It's here," said Becky. She pulled me off to the left, to where the cave narrowed into a slit.

"How could the creatures who live in this giant sector get through here?" I whispered.

"I don't know, but there's a portal." She pointed. I couldn't see it, but I had a feeling she was right. Maybe it was a light buzzing around me, or maybe it was just my imagination.

"Do you think it goes to the passage, or straight to their planet?" I asked.

"We don't have much choice," said Mom.

"Okay, then." Becky and I passed through the slit into the portal.

31

I STUMBLED, MY BODY buzzing with the shock of the portal, and tried to get my bearings. I was back in the passage. At least, I *thought* it was the passage. It had changed even more since the last time I'd been in it. Far from being its original pink, it was no longer even blotchy shades of pink and red. Instead, the entire misshapen tube was a pale, pulsing green. A glob of green goo fell on my shoulder from above. The whole ceiling was dripping, all the way along the passage.

I slipped on the gooey ground and stumbled into the far wall, only it was nothing like a wall anymore. It was soft and sticky, and my hands sank in.

Becky smashed against the wall next to me and screamed. Her arm and leg were inside a door, its insides swirling madly, expanding toward me. I pulled her out of the door, just in time to see Mom and Dad come through.

"Be careful!" I yelled.

Dad pulled Mom into the space between our door and the next. "Where are we going?"

"That way," said Becky, pointing to my left.

I opened my backpack a little, motioning for Becky to do the same with hers. "Are you all right?" The Brocine I was carrying were standing up, looking at me. The adult nodded. "Are yours all right?"

"Kind of," she said.

"Hang on, okay? It's going to be a rough ride."

The adult nodded again, and I closed the bag.

Tast-e burst through the door and nearly fell into me.

"Tell them to be careful of falling into these doors! They need to come one by one and follow us slowly!" I had to shout to be heard. A wind was blowing against my face, whooshing past my ears.

Tast-e put his head back through the portal.

Becky pushed past me and Mom and Dad, and we all started clomping slowly forward, our feet sinking in deep with every step. The wind was against us, making our progress even harder. The passage vibrated and hummed. A glob hit the side of my face. I reached up to wipe it away, but another glob fell on my head.

Dad slipped and fell forward, taking Mom with him. They scrambled to get up again. *Another* glob hit me on the chin. Thick, greenish liquid was now falling from the sky and spraying out from all the walls.

A Pipe Man appeared in a doorway just ahead of us on the right. It floated halfway through, thrust itself just past the doorway, and then was sucked back through the door. Another one appeared at the next door. It was sucked back before it even made it all the way through. I glanced behind me. Tast-e and Grav-e were now in the passage, followed by Ip, who was carrying Gript and pushing Hon-tri-bum forward, and then all of the Xaxor. We had made it through. But the Pipe Men weren't sticking to the bargain.

Another Pipe Man pushed through a door right between Becky and me, holding a calculator in its top-hole. Its three bottom eyes bent back toward the door, straining to blow out enough air to keep it in the same place. The top two eyes of another Pipe Man appeared through the door next to it, but it didn't seem to be able to get any farther. The sides of its top-hole smacked together.

"You're not scary!" Becky gave the Pipe Man between us a push between its fifth and sixth eyes.

It doubled over with a yelp and then, with a whoosh, was sucked back through the door. As the Pipe Man's last two eyes vanished, the calculator slipped out of its top-hole's grip. It fell to the gooey ground with a plop.

"I'm *not* infinitely sorry!" Becky cried. At the same time, I dropped to my knees and grabbed the calculator. Even if Becky thought she could figure the doors out, it would still come in handy.

A Xaxor leg wrapped around both the calculator and my hand.

"Come on, not now!" I tugged the calculator, but the Xaxor, who wasn't *our* Xaxor, held on. Everyone else had stopped behind us.

"You let go of it," said Dad to the Xaxor.

The rest of the Xaxor glared at me from behind all twelve of their eyes, which bulged out as their bodies strained against the wind.

"You owe it to *us*," said Tast-e, who appeared completely unfazed by the wind, even though it was blowing his plasticky blue hair against his skull.

I was acutely aware that Hon-tri-bum was watching me, too. But its bottom eyes were struggling so hard against the wind that it couldn't say whatever it was thinking. In fact, its whole body was pressed against Ip, as if without the Horn-Puff behind it, it would be blown down the passage.

Becky grabbed the calculator too. "We're not letting go," she said. We both pulled.

The Xaxor wrapped another leg around the calculator and pulled against us. My feet were slipping on the gooey ground, and I wasn't sure how long I could do this. Those Xaxor legs were really strong.

The calculator broke open with a pop. All three of us were still holding on to it, but there was now a gap running lengthwise between its two halves. Pink goo dripped from the hole, along with a thick greenish-brown mud.

"That goo — it's just like the passage before it turned green!" I said.

"I guess it makes sense," said Becky. "This stuff must make portals." She let go of the broken calculator, so I did, too.

The Xaxor held the device up to its eyes and pried the halves farther apart. That was when I remembered:

Front had said no one could ever see what was inside a calculator. But it was too late. Everyone had seen now. I just wondered why Front cared so much.

Hon-tri-bum shot forward on a burst of air, whooshing between Mom and Dad. Its top and bottom eyes leaned back in the wind. With much effort, it pushed its bottom two eyes forward, pointing its mouth up at me. "We protected you. We taught you. And you betrayed us. You helped the Frontringhor escape." The Pipe Man fell back against Dad.

"Why do you care about Front? It's just a zoo from like me," I said.

"You know nothing!" said Hon-tri-bum. Its voice was labored as it struggled to speak. "Why did it give you the calculator? Why did it imprint the device to you? To help you? No! It needed you to help these idiot Hottini create a rift!"

"How do you know any of that?"

Behind Hon-tri-bum and Mom and Dad, Grav-e and Tast-e conspicuously didn't look at each other. Great. I should have known they'd tell on us. I translated for Becky. "Glad you saved them now?"

But Becky didn't seem to care. She hopped up and down. "Ryan, you get it, right? You get it?"

"I get what?" I asked. The wind was just as harsh as ever. We should have been moving again instead of standing here. One of those Pipe Men was going to make it through a door soon.

"Front *is* the passage!"

"What?"

"He said they were inside him! And the Pipe Men are in here. He didn't want anyone to open a calculator, and it's got the same stuff inside as the passage. And the passage is nowhere. It's the place between all points. So he can be bigger inside than out!"

"No way! Becky says Front is the passage!" I tried to wrap my brain around this. I remembered how the passage had been changing, how it had felt and looked like flesh, how its floor had rearranged itself for me while Front was guiding me to the hospital door. And how Front had wanted to leave his planet, but the Pipe Men wouldn't let him.

"And you helped it!" Hon-tri-bum cried. "If it escapes, there will be no more space travel, except by spaceship. It will take lifetimes to get anywhere!"

"I'm right!" said Becky. "He said I'm right, didn't he?"

I translated.

Becky narrowed her eyes and pushed past me. She poked Hon-tri-þum between the eyes. "You're hurting him. That's why he's not pink anymore." She grabbed Hon-tri-þum around the middle and pulled him away from Dad.

"Becky, what are you doing?" Dad cried. "That's a Master!"

"He's not our master!" Becky pushed Hon-tri-þum toward the nearest door.

Hon-tri-þum's top three eyes fell into the portal, but it pushed out a gust of air beneath it, keeping its mouth visible. "May your eyes —" The rest of Hon-tri-þum was sucked away.

"Becky!" said Dad.

Everyone else stood still for a few seconds.

"Come on!" I yelled. The wind was getting even stronger. "We have to get out of here! Becky, where are we going? Where's Front's planet?"

"Here!" Becky sprang forward and began to run.

We all followed, our various From feet pounding into the ground, which I now knew was actually Front's flesh. And it was so green and gooey and sick. We had to help him, and not just because we still needed him to help us.

Becky stopped in front of a door. "Come on, before it changes!" She jumped through.

"Everyone, quick!" I waved at them, waited until it was clear that everyone had seen, then followed her. I fell about four eyes to the ground. The door was hanging in midair above me.

"Ryan, move!" Becky yelled.

I rolled out of the way. The wind was still blowing through the portal, sending debris whooshing around my head and shoulders. I was in a bog, and my hands and knees were rapidly sinking. I pushed against the soggy ground, trying not to jiggle my backpack too much, and struggled to mostly upright. My legs were sunk into the bog up to my calves. Mom and Dad dropped through the door.

"Mom, Dad, move!" Becky yelled.

As they rolled aside, out came Ip and Gript.

"Roll!" I yelled, getting my wits back.

Gript rolled out of the way just in time to avoid being tackled by Grav-e and Tast-e, who did not avoid getting trapped under a ball of many Xaxor. The Xaxor hummed, and the Hottini growled, and Gript squeaked. Ip sat up and began shaking with laughter.

At any other time, I probably would also have noticed

how funny it was to see the arrogant Hottini struggling to get the stinky Xaxor off their faces. But this wasn't the time. I had to make sure we were on Frontringhor. There was bog, bog, and more bog.

"Ryan, look!" Becky pointed behind me.

I struggled to turn myself around. There, only a few yards away, so close that I surely would have seen it at once if not for all the commotion, was a giant wall of blackness. The rift of variable infinity.

The five Xaxor, having finally gotten unwrapped from the Hottini, stood just out of the way of the swirling portal we'd fallen through. The Hottini stood up to their knees in bog, both watching the rift.

"Well, this is a sty on a fine eye," said Ip, who had stopped laughing. "Where are we supposed to go now?"

"How will we get home?" said Gript, at Ip's feet.

"We have to help Front," I said. "It can help us, but the Masters are hurting it. It must have gone through that!" I pointed at the rift. "Front!" I shouted. "Where are you? What's going on?"

The blackness of the rift rippled in front of us.

I took a step forward.

"Ryan!" Mom put a hand out to stop me.

"It's okay," I said, tossing her hand off. "It's just a big portal. I've seen one before." I walked right up to the blackness. "Front?"

The tip of an antenna appeared in front of me at knee level.

"Front, it's Ryan. And Becky's here." I waved at her.

She broke away from Dad and plopped down on her knees next to me. "Are you hurt?"

Another antenna slowly pushed through the portal, and both antennae reached down for the ground. They patted around the ground, finally reaching me, poking me in the leg.

I got down on my knees next to Becky, trying to ignore the way my hands and knees sank into the bog. "Front, tell us what we can do. How can we help you? What happened?"

The edge of Front's head appeared through the portal, then an inch, and then more, until his head dropped with a thump into the bog. One antenna stayed on my knee, but the other fell flat next to his head.

"Front? What happened to you?" Becky lifted Front's head in both hands and wiped the mud off of his mouth with her sleeve. The lips moved a little. "Front?" Becky rubbed the creature's head, wiping more mud off.

Very slowly, Front raised his head up and moved his lips.

We had to lean in very close to hear what he was saying.

"Help me," he whispered.

"We will," I said. "What can we do?"

"The Pipe Men are trying . . . to bring me back. They want to trap me here . . . forever." The limp antenna jerked.

"Where are they? What are they doing?"

"Outside."

"I don't understand."

"Get them off me. I can fight them inside. Just get them off me." Front's head collapsed again.

Becky gently laid it on the ground. "We have to go through the rift and help him," she said.

I imagined a planet full of Pipe Men, with wires and spaceships and weapons we didn't even know about. What could we do against an army of them? Still, I knew she was right. We had to help him. I nodded at her and put my hand on Front's head, feeling my way along the neck that stretched into the portal. The back of his body was rough, but also clammy, as though he had been sweating for some time. "Keep your hand on him," I said. "If there are too many, we have to come back, okay?"

She nodded.

"Too many what?" Mom demanded.

"Pipe Men," I said. "They're hurting him." I looked back at the rest of the Froms assembled in the bog. "The Masters are hurting it, and it's our only way back to our own planets. I don't know how many are out there, but we have to try. We have to do everything we can to save it."

There was silence for a few seconds.

"We have to go!" said Becky. "Look at him!"

"Take off your backpack. Gript? Can you watch your family? There's water here, at least."

Gript scampered forward as I opened Becky's and my backpacks and lifted the Brocine out one by one. Our Xaxor appeared next to us and began siphoning water from the bog into their listless mouths. "Go, Ry-an," said Gript. "We will follow." He looked around. "We all will, I know."

"You can't fight the Masters," said Dad. "How are you going to fight the Masters?"

"We just are," I said.

"Not with your little sister, you're not. Come here, Becky."

"We're going to fight them, and we're going to win," Becky cried, and ran through the rift.

"Becky!" I followed her, running on the other side of Front. I even got a few steps before I stopped to gasp at where we'd gone.

32

I WAS STARING AT EMPTY SPACE. Empty except for three giant spaceships looming in front of me, backed up by stars and galaxies, tiny points of light spread out forever. There was no planet beneath us, no planet close enough to be anything but a light in the distance.

I shouldn't have been able to breathe, but I could. I should have been floating weightless, but I wasn't. I was standing next to Front's body, which stretched out into space. For the first time, I could see all the way to the end of him, a tiny second head at the edge of blackness. I was on some kind of platform that extended from the underside of Front's body like a wing. It was almost completely clear but shimmered with a light pink color, just enough for me to see that it ended only three feet from Front's body. It was solid beneath my feet, but its edges were jagged, and beyond it there was nothing but space.

I pressed my chest against Front's body and wrapped both arms over his back. My hands barely reached past the middle of his five-foot-wide body. If something happened to the platform, if there was a wind, if anything went wrong at all, I could fall out into empty space. And I was pretty sure that whatever was making air and gravity around Front's body was *not* going to be out there. I willed myself to keep my eyes open. I couldn't panic.

Becky was standing on the other side of Front's body, hanging on, staring up at the spaceships. They were long and thin like the Pipe Men themselves, though each was larger than any of the ships I'd seen in the spaceport on O-thʊl-bə. Windows rose vertically up the sides, eye-shaped giant ovals shining dim light. The ships rose up in a pyramid shape above Front's body. Each had a hatch open where a Pipe Man's mouth would be, from which came two thick lines of deep black Pipe Man fabric. All six lines ended at Front, wrapping around him, cutting into his hide. They were taut, as if the Pipe Men were pulling him, but Front didn't move. His body was tense, fighting against them, shaking a little. The lines also cut right through whatever we were standing on, so that the wing-like platform had six three-inch-long holes. I did *not* like the idea that the only thing protecting me from empty space was fragile enough to be ruined by some Pipe Man fabric. *Breathe,* I told myself. But my vision blurred. I clung to Front's body for dear life.

Becky didn't look afraid at all. She was examining the setup, planning her move. Maybe she hadn't noticed that the lines were cutting into the platform. Maybe she didn't know as much about outer space as I did. But she had the right idea. Front was not going to let us fall. For some reason, we could walk and breathe, and I couldn't waste time thinking about it.

"We have to get these lines off him!" I called. Though Becky was only a few feet from me, my voice echoed back. Becky slid along her side of Front's body, still holding on, and I ran along mine. In a few seconds, I reached the first Pipe Man fabric line. Three inches wide and half an inch thick, it snaked around Front's body, cutting in. "Becky, get the line! It ends on your side! And watch the hole!"

She got to where I was and reached under Front.

"I'm getting it!" Her head disappeared from view. One second, two seconds, three seconds.

"Are you all right?" I looked up at the spaceships and couldn't believe what I saw. Out of each of the three open hatches, Pipe Men were coming down the lines. Holding on with skinny armlike assistants, they wore close-fitting black suits that left clear spaces for their eyes.

A Pipe Man was using assistant hands to slide down our line toward us, followed by two others, all watching me, sliding closer. They looked very alien in their space-suits.

"You don't want to come here!" I called. I made a kicking motion with my right leg, then jerked the line, hoping I could throw the Pipe Men off.

Becky emerged, grinning, holding the free end of the line. "The end of the line was wound around. But it wasn't a knot, it was just stuck like the bag Mom's cake came in!"

I grabbed the line from her and jerked it again. This time it was slack, and the jerking actually did something. The Pipe Men slid down the line too quickly. The first one caught itself with its assistant arms, and the next one crashed into the first one, then the next, until all three were smashed together, only inches from my face. Panicked, I let go of the line and pushed the closest Pipe Man. All three of them, clinging to the line, floated slowly away.

"Front must be making gravity!" Becky cried. "It doesn't work outside these wing thingies." She stomped on the ground to make her point.

"Watch that hole!" I cried. She was right, but the Pipe Men weren't helpless. There were still five more lines wrapped around Front, and Pipe Men were now sliding down all of them.

"Come on!" I called to Becky. "Let's get the next one!"

Front's whole back was clammy. As I ran along next to him, one hand tracing his back, the thick alien skin pulsed.

A scream came from behind me. Mom was standing just in front of the rift, staring at the scene with sheer terror.

"It's okay," I yelled, grabbing the next line. The ship attached to the line I'd tossed off was now pulling the line and its Pipe Men in. More Pipe Men lined the hatch, staring at us across the gap. We had to get the rest of the lines free before the Pipe Men could send out more.

Dad stepped halfway out of the rift, took one look, and pulled Mom back through.

The ship above and to the left of me thrust out a new line. It landed behind me with a smack, wrapped around Front's body, and dug in. Front thrashed weakly.

I slipped. My foot was half over the new hole in the platform. I wrapped my arms around Front for support and slid my foot back to solid ground.

"Take it!" Becky tossed me the line she'd just managed to release. I grabbed it and tossed it away, sending the two Pipe Men attached to it floating off. But at this rate, we'd never make any progress. We had to work faster.

Ip's head appeared through the portal, then his body. He stepped slowly out onto the shimmering platform and patted Front's back with an entire blobby arm. His pomegranate eyes took in the scene, focusing on the Pipe Man ships. He tested the platform, sticking one large leg out and tapping. "We'll get you out of this," Ip said, patting Front's back again. "Just hang on to us."

"Help us get these lines off! The Masters keep sending more!"

Ip stuck his head back through the portal. His horn shook. Then he turned around and blobbed toward the line the Pipe Men had just replaced. "I told them all they'd better help!" Ip called. He leaned backward over the place where the line was digging into Front's hide and, with a single swoop, dug his horn into the fabric and cut it in half. The line went flying out toward the spaceship, where a single Pipe Man who had begun the journey toward us floated helplessly just below the hatch.

Ahead of me, Pipe Men were crawling off the last three lines, using their spacesuits' assistant arms to pull themselves on top of Front's body. I counted eight. They struggled to stand, pushing with their new arms, wriggling inside their suits.

"They're not used to the gravity!" I shouted. "Their suits are meant for space!" I ran down the shimmering platform to the next line, where three Pipe Men hung on to Front, trying to pull themselves up, falling over each other.

Becky jumped on top of Front, landing on her belly.

She pushed one of the Pipe Men, and I pulled, and together we flung it past the platform and into space.

The other two jumped at us, but only managed to get a few inches off Front's body, pushing against the weight of their suits. Two more Pipe Men were crawling toward us, while the last three crawled away from us, toward Front's second head, which was upright, three antennae flailing.

"They're going to get him!" Becky cried. She pulled herself up and leapt over the two Pipe Men crawling toward us, running full speed over Front's body. Now I had four Pipe Men to deal with alone.

One of them managed to lift itself halfway up and leap toward me. I braced myself, but instead of me, it was the Pipe Man who was thrown backward, covered by the black, hairy body of a Xaxor. The Xaxor rolled, its legs wrapped around the Pipe Man, sending them both off Front's body past the jagged, shimmering edge.

I reached out for the Xaxor. "Grab on to me!"

It reached three legs out and wrapped them around my outstretched hands. I pulled, and as the Xaxor let go of the luckless Pipe Man, I fell back against Front, the Xaxor smashing against me.

Something whooshed past us with a tinny hum. I struggled to untangle myself from the Xaxor. With its body flattened against me, its heartbeat pumped into my ears. The heat of its body burned against my skin.

"It's okay. Front isn't going to let us fall." As long as we keep the Pipe Men from getting him, I thought. I tried to see where Becky was, but my view was blocked by a mess of Xaxor and Pipe Men, all struggling on top of Front. "They came!" I exclaimed.

Our Xaxor blinked at me, then jumped in to help its fellows. I ran toward Becky. She had knocked off one of the three Pipe Men, but the other two had grabbed her with their assistant arms, and she was clinging to Front, kicking and screaming at the top of her lungs.

I plucked an assistant from Becky's arm and kicked the Pipe Man it was attached to into space. Far behind me, Ip growled and a Pipe Man screeched, but the screech was abruptly cut off. I glanced back to see the Xaxor still fighting two Pipe Men. Beyond them, Ip stabbed a Pipe Man with his horn, and more Pipe Men were already floating in space. Ip had gotten all the Pipe Men on his end!

Grip was scampering down Front's body toward me. Dad stepped cautiously from the rift onto the platform and Mom, face white, followed him, holding all of Gript's children in her arms.

Lastly, Tast-e walked slowly out onto the platform, followed closely by Grav-e. They calmly took in the scene and exchanged a brief series of barks. Then Tast-e rushed forward, barreling toward a line that was just dropping three Pipe Men ahead of Ip. With a crash and a growl, Tast-e knocked all three of the Pipe Men out into space.

One Pipe Man was still clinging to Front's thin, tapering neck by one arm, holding Becky in the other. I crashed into its body as hard as I could, while Becky wrenched herself free.

"Yes!" Becky scrambled on top of Front, pumping her arms in victory.

Front's neck sagged and his three antennae drooped.

Becky's face fell. "Front? Are you all right?" She hugged his neck. His antennae twitched.

"We have to get the rest of them off," I said. "It's the only way to help him!" I grabbed her hand and turned to look back down Front's body.

All the Xaxor were hanging on to each other by their legs, making a haphazard, confused chain that contained two struggling Pipe Men. One Xaxor hung dangerously beyond Front's body, hugging itself with its legs. In the confusion, two of the Xaxor pushed a Pipe Man into space, leaving only one Pipe Man struggling to free itself from Xaxor legs. That was when I saw Ip.

Far down Front, he was hanging on by one blobby arm. A Pipe Man had its assistant arms wrapped around Ip's horn. It was attached to a line with two other Pipe Men on it, still hanging in space. Dad was leaning on Ip's arm, using his weight to hold Ip down.

"We have to help Ip!" I cried.

Becky raced behind me on the platform.

I reached Ip, panting, and grabbed the assistant arms around his horn. At the same time, the line tugged its Pipe Men back, pulling on Ip's horn.

Ip wailed.

Becky kicked the Pipe Man holding Ip's horn while I kept pulling its assistant arms. Finally, I wrenched the arms free, and Becky and I pushed the Pipe Man away, expecting it and its fellows to float away helplessly, but it didn't work. Their ship was closer now, and it somehow was exerting force on the line to keep the Pipe Men only a few eyes away. They kept reaching, falling back toward us.

Both of the bottom two ships were bearing down on

us from above, their hatch-mouths gaping open, Pipe Men waiting in rows, slowly but surely about to reach us.

"Go float!" Becky yelled. She kicked one of the Pipe Men as it reached toward her. The Pipe Man fell back, but it managed to grab Becky's foot with its assistant arm. It pulled her away from us.

"Becky!" I reached for her arm, but she slid away from me.

Dad jumped after her, and I jumped after him. Dad grabbed her arms, and I hit the platform behind him, clutching his legs. The Pipe Man and its line tried to drag us all off the platform, but Dad and I pulled back. Becky's head and shoulders were still with us, but her legs were kicking around in space. Both Dad's head and mine were also past where the platform used to be, but the edge of it expanded under us, shimmering and jagged and looking more fragile than ever.

Come on, Front, I thought. *Hang on to her. Don't let her go.*

The jagged edges of the platform shifted. Front must have been trying to keep us all in his zone of power, but how long could he do it? Tiny holes opened beneath my chest, then closed again.

"Now, son! Pull!" Dad shouted.

We both pulled with all our strength. Becky snapped free of the Pipe Man, and we all fell against Front. I stood up just in time to see Tast-e head-butting a Pipe Man out into space, back near Front's second head. At the same time, Gript released a line and sent three Pipe Men flailing. All five Xaxor bounced on top of Front's body, humming.

"Yes!" Becky and I cried together.

"We did it!" Ip punched his blobby fist into the air.

Front, free of his lines, began to drop away from the Pipe Men ships. At first he dropped slowly, but then he fell faster and faster. My stomach was reeling, and all I could do was hang on. Several Pipe Men, still attached to their lines, became smaller and smaller. Front rippled as we fell, shaking with some colossal effort.

"The rift," I gasped.

"It's still there!" cried Becky.

I raised my head just enough to see it, a shimmering blackness with a hint of red inside. Was it falling through space with us, or was it big enough to cover all this distance? "We can go back through it."

"Will it go back to Frontringhor?"

"Front!" I cried out. I had no idea if Front could hear me. "The rift! Go back through it! You have to stop dropping! We can't take it!" Ip was slumped over Front's body, and I felt like doing the same. Mom was clinging to Dad, pressing Gript's family tightly against her chest. Front was too big around to properly hold on to. We were sucked into him only by his own force, and I wasn't sure it would last much longer.

"His head!" said Becky, pointing at the head floating in space. "We have to make sure it's awake!"

I pulled myself onto Front's body and helped Becky up. We had to climb over the unconscious Ip, past a ball of tangled Xaxor, and Grav-e and Tast-e, who were hanging on by their front legs, blue hair sticking straight up. We crawled toward Front's head, which was hanging so low that all I could see was his thin neck. Front's body was even more slippery than before. We slipped and slid, but managed to make our way to where his head drooped unconscious, all three antennae hanging low.

"Front," I shouted. "Front, wake up!" I held his head, and Becky gently lifted all three of his antennae.

"It's me, Becky." She drew the antennae along her face.

"Front, please," I pleaded. "We need you with us. We need you to crawl back through the rift. We need to stop falling."

Front's head moved a little, and one of his antennae twitched.

"Come on, wake up," Becky whispered.

Front's mouth didn't move, but I still heard his voice, very quiet, almost too quiet to hear. *"Ryan."*

Far down his body, I could see the others still hanging on, smashed against him. It seemed like we were not dropping as quickly anymore, that the others were not quite as distressed. But what would happen if Front died right here in space with all of us on him? Would we still have air and gravity? Would we have any way to get back home? Would we keep dropping forever?

Dad was waving from the other end of Front's body, calling out something, but I was too far away to hear.

"Front, come on, you have to go back through the rift. Take all of us through or we're going to die here."

Two of Front's antennae twitched.

"Becky!" I cried. "Go down to the other head and wake it up. He's not all here without it. Both ends are going to have to move!"

Becky didn't argue. She ran along the platform until she reached the others.

Dad and Ip and our Xaxor converged on her, but after a few seconds, they let her through. She scrambled over Front's body and disappeared again into the rift.

"Front!" I tapped him lightly on the side of his head.

His mouth twitched, then turned upward into a smile. "Ryan," he said again, this time out loud. His voice was very soft, and I had to lean in close to hear him. "Thank you."

"You're welcome, Front," I said. "Anything you need, but you have to get us back through the rift!"

"I'm going to get you home, Ryan," said Front. As he said it, our progress through space slowed. Then it came to a complete stop.

Far away, Gript was looking toward me, perched on top of Ip's head. In front of Ip, the rest of the Xaxor were still all bunched up together. Closer to me, Grav-e and Tast-e stood on the left side of Front's body, both staring the same direction into space.

I looked where they were looking, at the patterns of stars in the endless expanse. I might never see this again, might never be out in space again at all, anywhere. I took a deep breath, trying to quiet the shaking that had started out of nowhere. All of a sudden, I didn't want to go back through the rift. I didn't want this all to end. But I could feel us moving, though our tiny movement made no difference in the view before us.

Mom and Dad disappeared, then Ip, Gript, the Xaxor, and the Hottini, until it was only Front and me, slowly heading for the rift. I put my hand on the top of Front's head. "Thank you," I said.

Front wrapped an antenna around my arm as we slowly slid into the rift. The last thing I saw was a cluster of stars in the black sky, worlds too far to fly to in a lifetime, but still somehow right next to us.

33

THE SPRAY HIT ME LIKE A dozen hammers. I fell backward off Front and splashed into the water, then flailed my way upright. There was water everywhere, except for Front, floating on top of it, and my friends and family splashing around him.

Front's head was still, his three antennae lying slack in the water.

I got one arm around his body to hold myself up and lifted his head with the other. "Front! Wake up! You'll drown!"

Front's head did not move, but I still heard his voice. *"I will not drown, Ryan. You do not need to worry about me. Let me sink."*

"Not yet," I cried. "We have to get everyone home!" I let Front's head down gently until it reached the water and slowly sank. His body was still floating high enough for me to hang on to.

Half of Front's body length away, Grav-e and Tast-e were treading water, while Ip lifted a wilted Xaxor onto Tast-e's back. Grav-e was already covered with three of the soggy buglike Froms.

Gript was on top of Front, huddled with his children.

Mom, looking drenched, held on to Front next to Gript and his family, and as I watched, Dad burst through the surface. He pulled a Xaxor from the water behind him and passed it to Ip, who set it carefully on top of Tast-e.

Becky came into view from behind Front's other head and clambered on top of him, dripping. She waved at me.

Hanging on to Front, I made my way down his side. As I got closer, I could hear what she was saying.

"We're on Earth, Ryan!" She pointed at the sky. "Look!"

A few clouds rolled by, but the sky was mainly blue. There was only one sun and nothing else above us. Water stretched out in all directions.

"There are probably lots of other planets with oceans," I said.

"*It is Earth,*" said Front's voice. "*I promised I would get you home. I have closed all my portals everywhere. You will be safe from the Pipe Men.*"

"All of them?" I asked. "What about the rift? And the tunnels through space?"

"*There are no rifts without me,*" said Front. "*There are no tunnels. I have closed everything. That is why I am so sick. Once I went through the rift, I began closing them all. And now, I am finished. Thank you, Ryan and Becky. At great risk to yourselves, you have set me free. I will never forget it.*"

"I don't understand," I said. "How could they trap you?"

"*When they came to Frontringhor, I did not know what I was. I had lived my whole life, many thousands of your years, without ever knowing there was more in the universe than me. One day my insides began to burn. The Pipe Men came, telling me they could help me, teach me. I did not know they were the cause of my pain, that they were inside me. But I learned. I listened to their thoughts, began to feel the truth of my own body, to understand what I am.*"

"What are you?" I asked. Right now, he looked like a big, soggy, sick animal. I rubbed a hand along his back, feeling the wet, thick, sweaty hide.

"I am . . ." he paused. "There is no Earth word for what I am. I am the place between all points. I am not here in your universe." He paused again, leaving the channel to his mind open, giving the impression of listening to his mental breath. "I am like another universe. One that is everywhere in your universe, but no particular place. I was tied to this universe only by my planet, Frontringhor. And now I am free. I am sorry if I cannot explain."

"But if you're so big, how could the Pipe Men keep you?" asked Becky. "Why couldn't you just open a rift and leave?" She laid her wet cheek against Front's body.

"I tried to open bigger doors," said Front. "But each time I would open one, they would steal flesh from my insides and mud from my planet. They used my own body and my home against me to close them. As long as I was on Frontringhor, I could not expel them. I needed a rift of variable infinity. They are unpredictable, moving through space and changing quickly. It was the only portal so complex that the Pipe Men would not be able to control it, and I could not make it by myself. That is why I changed the door you hid behind so that it would lead to Frontringhor. That is *why I gave you the calculator, Ryan. That is why I asked you to open a portal from Brock. I knew the Hottini were close to discovering me. They had the power to interfere with your portal, and the ambition to attempt it. I set the calculator to help me cause a rift when it was interfered with. I am sorry I could not tell you. I could not risk the Pipe Men learning."*

"It's all right," I said. "You helped us save our dad."

"You have helped me far more than I have helped you," said Front. *"Leaving Frontringhor was only the first step. You helped me escape their spaceships. I am very tired, but for the first time since they came, I am no longer in pain."*

"What if they come back?" Becky asked, squeezing Front's back. "They still have the calculators." She looked at me, eyes tearing up. She was right. The Pipe Men could just open a portal and find him.

"Don't worry, Becky," said Front. *"The calculators are tied to my planet as well as to me. They are made of my flesh and its earth, and they need power from us both together. That is why I had to get away, no matter how much I love my planet. The calculators will never work again unless I go back home. No one will ever use me again. No one will come inside me unless I want it."* I thought I heard a smile in his voice.

"Are you going to stay with us?" asked Becky.

"I will be here until I get my strength back," said Front. *"I have never been through such a thing, so I can't say how long it will be."*

"Can you still open portals?" I asked. "Just to get everyone home?"

"I will try," said Front. *"But I do not have much longer. I must sink to the bottom and sleep for a long time."*

"We must send the Xaxor first," said Tast-e. "They will die if we can't get them dry."

One of the Xaxor on Tast-e's back twitched a leg, then wilted deeper into the others.

A portal opened just above the water.

Ip, who could float and who swam gracefully, despite his large, blobby body, lifted one Xaxor and then another, passing them through the portal.

"Wait!" I cried, splashing over to them. "Where is ours?"

"He tricked us twice!" said Becky. "Send him back!"

"He didn't," I said. "Or maybe he did, I don't know. But they helped us fight off the Pipe Men. They didn't sell us after all, did they?"

Our Xaxor was the last one left, sitting on top of Grav-e. It flailed its legs and lifted its body partially upright, so it could look at me with all three eyes. It looked sad and sick, wilted with water, but its eyes were clear enough.

"Goodbye, Xaxor," I said. "I believe you about not wanting to hurt us, and thank you for helping."

The Xaxor reached a leg out and gently brushed my face. Then it blinked all three eyes at me slowly. *"Thank you, Earth,"* said its voice, distant and quiet in my head, as if through a great empty distance. *"It has been fun."*

Ip lifted the Xaxor and gently pushed it through the portal. The door closed.

"You'd better get the Brocine home next," said Tast-e. "They need fresh water."

"Can you do one right by you?" I asked.

A tiny portal opened right next to Front's body, where Gript sat with Mom and his family.

I swam back to them. "Goodbye, Gript! Thank you for everything, and good luck."

"Go safely, Ry-an," said Gript. "Without you, my children would not have survived. If we can ever help you in any way, we will."

Becky picked Gript up and hugged him close.

The little Brocine squirmed, pulling his nose away, but laughed at the same time.

Mom gently picked up one of the adult children and passed her through the portal, following with the others, one by one.

Gript bowed to her, then to Becky, waved at me with a toothy grin, and followed. The portal snapped shut.

"Who's next?" I said, looking around. Only Ip and the two Hottini were left.

"Ip can't leave!" Becky cried. She leaned over Front's body and held her arms out.

Ip swam over and wrapped a wet, blobby arm around her, pulling her into the water. She climbed onto his shoulders. "You have a nice planet," Ip said. "Much like Hdkowl before the Masters came, with this beautiful water. But I have to go home. I'll find some way to see you."

I translated. I didn't know how he could possibly do that, since Front had closed up all the portals, but I didn't say anything. Becky knew all that anyway.

"Come on, stay with us!" she said. "We'll have lots of fun! I'll take you out in the yard every night!"

I translated.

"Someday," said Ip.

"At least wait," Becky insisted. "Leave last!"

"All right," said Ip. "Let our friends go first."

Becky leaned over Ip's shoulders toward the Hottini. "I'll . . ." She struggled for the words. "Miss you, too."

Grav-e's mouth twitched, revealing the closest thing to a real smile I'd seen on a Hottini. "It's been a pleasure," he said. Then he nodded deeply at Front's floating body. "And we must thank the Frontringhor. With you hiding on Earth, the Masters are no longer Masters. To think that all of space travel has depended on a single From for all these years! Even we Hottini have much to learn."

"I must thank you," said Front's voice.

Grav-e eyed the floating creature. "Though we did not know we were helping you," he said, "we are glad to have played a role in obtaining your freedom."

"I am sorry about your planet," said Front. *"I hope there was no permanent damage."*

"There was not," said Tast-e. "The Masters"— Tast-e nodded at me—"or rather, the Pipe Men, assisted us. I hope you are also safe."

"They will not find me," said Front. *"Once you all have left, there will be no more portals until I have recovered and I am ready."*

"As it should be," said Grav-e. "Goodbye, Frontringhor. Goodbye, Ry-an. Goodbye, Beck-y." Grav-e nodded ever so slightly to each of us and then swam into the portal that appeared hovering above the water.

"Go safely," said Tast-e, nodding just as slightly at me.

"And hold your eyes still," I said.

Tast-e nodded again, taking a last look at all of us and at the ocean, and then swam after Grav-e. The portal closed so abruptly, it nearly caught the very end of Tast-e's tail.

"Are you tired, Front?" asked Becky. "Maybe you can't send Ip back!"

"I can handle it," said Front softly. His voice now seemed to come from very far.

Dad was now hanging on to Front next to Ip, who still had Becky on his shoulders. "Come on, honey, get back on the big From." He reached out his arms to help her.

Becky gave Ip a long squeeze around his head.

Ip's horn shook, making ripples in the water.

Crying, Becky accepted Dad's help and climbed down onto Front, who was now sunk so low that water was lapping over his back even in the calm sea.

"Thank you for taking care of my family," said Dad.

"We will never forget it." Dad gripped Ip's arm, and Ip smiled, rolling his large eyes to take us all in.

"It's been quite a ride!" he said. "Thanks to you all, we will be able to free our home of the Masters. Come here." Ip reached out an arm to me.

I swam into it, holding back tears myself.

"You've got quite a child, Oscar," said Ip.

"I know," said Dad.

Ip patted Front. "I knew you'd get free someday," said Ip. "Thank you for taking us all with you."

"It was my pleasure, friend," said Front.

Another portal opened.

Ip opened his giant, wet, blobby arms, and we all fell into them, before he swam out of sight, his horn shaking in the water.

34

MOM, DAD, BECKY, AND I sat on top of Front, trying to stay out of the water. Luckily, the sun was still high in the sky, but we were all shivering from being soaked through.

"Can you open one last portal, Front?" I asked.

"I can handle one more, Ryan," said Front. *"But after this, I will be gone for a long time."*

"I don't want to go home," said Becky.

"Where else should we go, honey?" asked Mom.

"I don't know—somewhere else. Anywhere! We could go to Gript's planet, or Ip's planet."

"It won't be that bad," I said. "We can go to school like everyone else now. We can go outside, wear normal clothes. We won't have to hide anymore." Even as I said it, though, I wasn't sure if I wanted to go home either. I thought about the cashier at the store, the po-liceman.

"You'll get used to it," said Dad. "We all will. It will just take a little time." He put his arm around Becky and pulled her close.

"We're never going to see the Pipe Men again," Becky sobbed. "We're never going to go anywhere or meet any other Froms. We're only going to see stupid Earth people for the rest of our lives!"

"There must be a few Pipe Men still on Earth," said Mom. "Who knows what they'll do now that the portals are closed."

"Really?" Becky sniffed, but smiled a little. "We can find them and they can still teach me to speak Pipe Man!"

"We'll see, honey," said Mom.

"Don't cry, Becky," said Front, his voice even farther off now. *"I'll be better someday. For you, I'll open a portal again. I just need to rest for a while."*

"Do you mean it?" She pulled away from Dad and sank her arms into the water, wrapping them around Front's body.

A portal popped open only a few feet from her head. Its edges were indistinct, and it swirled crookedly.

"This should take you near your house," said Front. It was the tiniest whisper.

"Come on, honey," said Mom.

Becky kept sobbing. "How are we going to find you?"

"I'll find you," Front whispered.

"Find me as soon as you can!" She hugged him one more time, and then Dad picked her up and, splashing, carried her through the portal.

Mom jumped into the water and reached out her hand to me.

"I wish I still had the calculator," I said. "I wish I had something to remember you by."

"I won't forget, Ryan. When I am well..." He sank an inch deeper in the water. *"When I am well, we will go out again together."*

I took Mom's hand and let her help me, until I was sloshing into my own backyard, which was now muddy with salt water. Mom and I joined Dad and Becky, and we all stood huddled together in the twilight, watching the last portal sputter shut.